Women of Achievement

Nancy Pelosi

Women of Achievement

Susan B. Anthony

Hillary Rodham Clinton

Marie Curie

Ellen DeGeneres

Nancy Pelosi

Rachael Ray

Eleanor Roosevelt

Martha Stewart

Women of Achievement

Nancy Pelosi

POLITICIAN

Hal Marcovitz

NANCY PELOSI

Chelsea House
An imprint of Infobase Publishing
132 West 31st Street
New York NY 10001

Library of Congress Cataloging-in-Publication Data
Marcovitz, Hal.
Nancy Pelosi: Politician / Hal Marcovitz.
p. cm. — (Women of achievement)
Includes bibliographical references and index.
ISBN 978-1-60413-075-1 (hardcover)
1. Pelosi, Nancy, 1940—Juvenile literature. 2. Women legislators—United States—Biography—Juvenile literature. 3. Legislators—United States—Biography—Juvenile literature. 4. United States. Congress. House—Speakers—Biography—Juvenile literature. I. Title.
E840.8.P37M373 2009
328.73092—dc22
[B]

2008034674

Chelsea House books are available at special discounts when purchased in bulk quantities for businesses, associations, institutions, or sales promotions. Please call our Special Sales Department in New York at (212) 967-8800 or (800) 322-8755.

You can find Chelsea House on the World Wide Web at http://www.chelseahouse.com

Series design by Erik Lindstrom
Cover design by Ben Peterson

Printed in the United States of America

Bang EJB 10 9 8 7 6 5 4 3 2 1

This book is printed on acid-free paper.

All links and Web addresses were checked and verified to be correct at the time of publication. Because of the dynamic nature of the Web, some addresses and links may have changed since publication and may no longer be valid.

CONTENTS

Madam Speaker

When President George W. Bush strode into the crowded chamber of the U.S. House of Representatives in January 2007 to deliver the State of the Union address, the sergeant at arms uttered eight words that had never been heard in the history of the United States: "Madam Speaker, the president of the United States."[1]

Indeed, never in American history had the president entered a House chamber under the leadership of a woman. Three weeks before the president's address, the new Democratic Party majority in the House elected Representative Nancy Pelosi of California as speaker, the highest position in the chamber. As Bush took his place on the rostrum of the House, he was quick to acknowledge the historical significance of the moment. "Tonight," he said,

"I have the high privilege and distinct honor of my own as the first president to begin the State of the Union Message with these words: 'Madam Speaker.' "[2]

Pelosi, sitting behind the president on the speaker's dais, showed no emotion as Bush began to speak. Bush and Pelosi had long been adversaries, and she was concerned that a frown or other sour look on her face would be caught by the TV cameras, prompting viewers at home to find her disrespectful of the president. Before the speech, she told reporters, "We always give the president a warm welcome as our guest in the chamber."[3]

Still, as Bush addressed the nation and Pelosi sat silently behind him, there was no question that the American political landscape had undergone a dramatic change, and not just because a woman was now presiding over the U.S. House of Representatives.

FEW WOMEN IN CONGRESS

Just a year before, the Republican Party had been riding a wave of popularity that had helped its leaders remain in power for many years. In the House, the GOP—as the party is sometimes known—had sustained its control of the chamber for 12 years. Republicans controlled the Senate as well. In the meantime, Bush, a Republican, captured the White House in two closely fought and controversial elections. Throughout this period, the fortunes of the Democratic Party eroded as it struggled to define its objectives and find new leaders.

One such leader had quietly been climbing the ranks in Congress, becoming more and more influential within her party. Pelosi entered Congress in 1987. In 2001, she was elected Democratic whip, making her the second-highest officeholder within her party's caucus in the House. In 2002, the influence of Democrats in the House eroded further as the party registered losses in that year's elections.

President George W. Bush handed copies of his speech to Vice President Dick Cheney and House Speaker Nancy Pelosi before his State of the Union address on January 23, 2007, on Capitol Hill. When Bush entered the House chamber for his speech, the sergeant at arms uttered words never heard before: "Madam Speaker, the president of the United States."

As a result, Minority Leader Richard Gephardt resigned under pressure from caucus members. Gephardt failed to define a mission for the Democratic caucus in the House and came under criticism from many members of his party when he helped the Bush administration draft the House resolution authorizing the use of force against Iraqi dictator Saddam Hussein. When Gephardt stepped aside in late

2002, Pelosi campaigned hard and won the post of minority leader. She was now the top Democrat in the House and, in fact, the first woman to hold such a high position in the leadership of Congress.

Since the Congress was established under Article I of the U.S. Constitution in 1787, few women have served in either the House or the Senate. In fact, under the Constitution, women did not even receive the right to vote

DID YOU KNOW?

Nancy Pelosi's election as the first female speaker of the U.S. House marked a milestone in the struggle by women for equality in American politics. Other women have also made a difference:

- The first woman to run for Congress was Elizabeth Cady Stanton of New York, who sought a seat in 1866. At the time, New York law did not permit women to vote, so Stanton could not vote for herself.
- Victoria Claflin Woodhull was the first woman to run for president; in 1872, she campaigned as the nominee of the Equal Rights Party. Her running mate was Frederick Douglass, the former slave and noted civil-rights leader. Woodhull finished well behind the winner of the election, Republican Ulysses S. Grant.
- Jeannette Rankin was the first woman to win a seat in Congress when she was elected in 1916 to represent Montana.
- At the age of 87, Rebecca Felton became the first woman to serve in the U.S. Senate; she was appointed in 1922 by the governor of Georgia to fill a vacancy.
- The first woman elected to the Senate was Hattie Wyatt Caraway of Arkansas, who took her seat following the 1932 election.

until 1920, although by then many states had provided suffrage to women. In 1914, Montana approved voting rights for women, and two years later voters in that state sent the first woman to Congress, Jeannette Rankin, who took her seat in the House. Seventy-three years later, when Pelosi arrived in Washington to represent her Northern California congressional district, she was one of 22 women in the 435-member House. By 2006, the number of women

- In 1933, President Franklin D. Roosevelt appointed Frances Perkins as secretary of labor, making her the first woman to serve in a presidential Cabinet.
- Shirley Chisholm of Brooklyn, New York, was the first African-American woman elected to Congress. She took her seat following the 1968 election; four years later, she ran for president in several Democratic primaries.
- In 1981, Sandra Day O'Connor was appointed to the U.S. Supreme Court, making her the first woman to serve on the nation's highest court.
- Geraldine Ferraro, a member of the U.S. House of Representatives from New York, was the first woman to run for vice president on a major-party ticket; Ferraro and presidential candidate Walter Mondale lost the 1984 election to President Ronald Reagan and Vice President George H.W. Bush.
- In 1997, President Bill Clinton named Madeleine Albright the first female secretary of state.
- Condoleezza Rice was the first woman to be named national security advisor, appointed by President George W. Bush following the 2000 election; later, Bush appointed Rice secretary of state.

in the House had grown to 70. Meanwhile, just 14 women served in the 100-member Senate.

According to Ellen Malcolm, the president of EMILY's List, a political action committee that raises money for women who support abortion rights to run for office (EMILY means "Early Money Is Like Yeast—it grows"), many women have been kept out of Congress for years because few incumbents are defeated in their re-election campaigns. Since most incumbents are men, Malcolm says, there are few opportunities for women to take seats in Washington. "The biggest obstacle women candidates face is not about gender, it's about the lack of opportunity," Malcolm said. "Ninety-eight percent of incumbents who run for re-election are re-elected in most years. The bottom line is there are few opportunities."[4]

Given the sparse number of women elected to Congress since Rankin entered the House nearly a century ago, there could be no arguing with the historical significance of Pelosi's rise in the House leadership. As developments occurred in 2006, though, it soon became clear that the year would be unlike most others in Washington and that events would enable Pelosi to assume a much more significant position of leadership.

WEARY OF WAR AND SCANDAL

By 2006, Americans had grown weary of the war in Iraq. The conflict had cost the lives of nearly 3,000 American troops. As the men and women of the Army and Marines patrolled the country, they constantly found themselves targeted by terrorists. What's more, TV news broadcasts and other media reported horrific acts of violence on the streets of Baghdad and other Iraqi cities, where suicide bombers took the lives of dozens or hundreds of innocent civilians. The war had been popular at the outset, but as the 2006 elections approached, it was clear that most Americans wanted to bring the troops home. As a result, Bush's popularity eroded as he kept admonishing Americans to be patient, promising a more stable situation in Iraq.

Meanwhile, support for the Republican leadership in Washington had fallen as well, partly because of the GOP's support for the war but also because several Republicans found themselves caught up in a series of scandals. Among those scandals were the influence-peddling allegations brought against lobbyist Jack Abramoff. Lobbyists are hired by industry organizations, trade unions, and other special-interest groups to influence legislation. (The term stems from the nineteenth-century practice by the hired representatives to wait for members of Congress in the lobbies of Washington hotels, where they would present their arguments to the representatives and senators.) Lobbyists do serve a purpose, making it clear to members of Congress how legislation would affect their clients. In Abramoff's case, however, he was found to be providing members with excessive gifts and vacations to gain their support for his clients' interests. Abramoff eventually pleaded guilty to corruption charges and was sentenced to six years in prison. Several other people, including congressional aides, White House staff members, and other lobbyists, were also convicted in the scandal, as was U.S. Representative Robert Ney of Ohio, a Republican who was sentenced to 30 months in prison.

Another scandal that surfaced during the year involved allegations of sexual solicitation of teenagers by Republican Representative Mark Foley of Florida. The teenagers worked as pages, or messengers, in the House and Senate. Foley resigned after evidence surfaced indicating he had sent sexually suggestive e-mails to current and former pages.

In the fall 2006 election, voters reacted decisively against Bush, the war, and the Republican scandals, delivering new majorities in both the House and the Senate to the Democrats. In the case of the House, the victory meant that the minority leader, Pelosi, would now move up to speaker—the most important position in the chamber.

MARBLE CEILING

As with all leadership positions in Congress, the speaker is elected by the other members of the House. The speaker wields enormous power, making committee assignments and appointing the chairs of the committees. Also, the speaker has tremendous influence over the agenda of the House and is able to initiate legislation and decide which bills come to the floor for a full vote of the chamber. The Constitution recognizes the importance of the speaker by placing the officeholder second in line to the presidency, meaning that, in the event the president and vice president are disabled or otherwise unable to serve, the speaker becomes president. As the leader of the Democratic caucus, Pelosi's election as speaker was guaranteed.

On January 4, 2007, Pelosi accepted the gavel as the first woman to serve as speaker of the U.S. House of Representatives. The first day of a new congressional term always begins with a swearing-in ceremony. Many members bring their children onto the floor with them so that they can share the experience with their families. When Pelosi prepared to take the oath as speaker, the grandmother of six invited all the children in the House chamber onto the dais. "This is an historic moment," she declared. "It's an historic moment for the Congress. It's an historic moment for the women of America. It's a moment for which we have waited for over 200 years."[5]

Moments later, in her first speech presiding over the House, Pelosi talked about breaking the "marble ceiling"—a reference to the "glass ceiling" that many women in business are unable to penetrate. The glass ceiling refers to the office of the corporate president—a place women

As the newly sworn-in speaker of the House, Nancy Pelosi waved the speaker's gavel, surrounded by children and grandchildren of House members. In her first speech as speaker, on January 4, 2007, Pelosi talked of breaking through the "marble ceiling" in Washington.

can see above them but in many cases are unable to break into. In Washington, where the historic federal buildings are constructed of marble, Pelosi's reference to the marble ceiling meant that women had now broken through a previously impenetrable barrier and were now able to hold the most important positions of power—speaker of the House, the post of majority leader in the Senate, and the presidency itself. She said:

> Never losing faith, we waited through the many years of struggle to achieve our rights. But women

> weren't just waiting; women were working. Never losing faith, we worked to redeem the promise of America, that all men and women are created equal. For our daughters and granddaughters, today we have broken the marble ceiling. For our daughters and our granddaughters, the sky is the limit; anything is possible for them.[6]

REINING IN THE PRESIDENT

A few weeks later, as Bush delivered the State of the Union address, it was clear that the Congress was divided, particularly when he discussed the war in Iraq. Even members of the Republican caucus had been calling on Bush to find a way to wind down the American commitment to Iraq. Instead, the president declared his intentions to follow through with a plan to increase the number of troops in Iraq. "Many in this chamber understand that America must not fail in Iraq because you understand the consequences of failure would be grievous and far-reaching," Bush said. "If American forces step back before Baghdad is secure, the Iraqi government would be overrun by extremists on all sides."[7]

As Bush spoke those words, many Republicans stood to applaud the president, but many members of his party also stayed in their seats and did not applaud. A majority of Democrats in the room refused to applaud as well. Afterward, Pelosi and Harry Reid, the new majority leader of the Senate, issued a joint statement, making it clear that the Congress was no longer going to give a free hand to Bush in Iraq. "While the president continues to ignore the will of the country, Congress will not ignore this president's failed policy," Pelosi and Reid said in their statement. "His plan will receive an up-or-down vote in both the House and Senate, and we will continue to hold him accountable for changing course in Iraq."[8]

Born into Politics

Everybody who lived in Baltimore's Little Italy in the 1940s and 1950s knew the D'Alesandros. The family's modest home on Albemarle Street was like a "little city hall." Every day, friends, neighbors, and total strangers knocked on the door and hoped that Thomas J. D'Alesandro Jr.—"Tommy the Elder" to most everyone—would find a way to help them with their troubles.

Tommy D'Alesandro had been helping his neighbors since 1928, when he was elected to his first political office—a seat in the state legislature. Since then, he won many elections for more important seats—positions in city council and Congress, among others. In 1947, D'Alesandro won the first of his three terms as mayor of Baltimore.

He owed much of his political career to the "favor file"—a metal filing cabinet he kept at home filled with thousands of index cards in which he carefully recorded the names of constituents who had come to him over the years for favors and how he had met his constituents' needs. Did a constituent need a job? Mayor D'Alesandro found him work in the parks department. Did a merchant complain about a cracked sidewalk in front of his store? The mayor responded by sending out a crew to patch the cracks. Was the rubbish piling up in the street? A city trash truck was dispatched immediately. Were rowdies making trouble in front of a block of stores? Mayor D'Alesandro doubled the police patrols.

When Election Day rolled around, Mayor D'Alesandro knew he could count on the people whose names were in the favor file to return his favors and provide him with their votes. Shortly before the election, the newer names in the favor file were sure to receive a phone call or a knock on the door, nudging them with gentle reminders about the mayor's favors and the need to give Tommy the Elder, or his candidates, their votes.

Nancy Patricia D'Alesandro was born into the family of Baltimore's most renowned politician on March 26, 1940, the youngest of six children and only daughter to Tommy and Annunciata D'Alesandro. As she grew older, "Little Nancy" was put to work by her father in the front parlor of the house on Albemarle Street. She answered the door, welcomed the mayor's constituents into the house, listened to their problems, and then guided them into their meetings with her father. "Politics was a way of life for us," Pelosi said. "I saw my parents as working the side of the angels. They were doing good stuff for the underdogs. I learned from them that politics is a noble calling, that we have a responsibility to other people. And I learned how to count the votes. If you don't have the votes, it doesn't work."[1]

Pelosi learned a lot of lessons about politics from her father. Years later, after she arrived in Congress, Pelosi started to keep her own favor file.

HIGH SCHOOL VALUES

For a politician's family, there was always plenty to do, especially as an election neared. The mayor sent his sons and daughter into the neighborhoods to help turn out the vote. Later, his eldest son, Thomas III—"Tommy the Younger"—followed his father into politics and served a term as mayor himself. At home, Nancy and her brothers stuffed political literature into envelopes, then fanned out into the neighborhoods to drop them into people's doors.

Nancy's mother may have been the family's hardest worker. Annunciata held fund-raisers at St. Leo's, the D'Alesandro family church. She also gathered women from the Baltimore neighborhoods into the basement of the Albemarle Street home, where she lectured them about the importance of voting. Pelosi believed that her mother wished to run for public office herself—Annunciata often studied law books in her spare time—but stepped aside in deference to her husband's career. Also, back in the 1940s and 1950s, few women were making it in politics, particularly in the rough-and-tumble world of city politics in Baltimore. Said Pelosi, "As first lady of Baltimore, my mother . . . showed me what a significant role women could play in politics, as she worked hand in hand with my father to serve the people of Baltimore."[2]

Nancy spent her high school years at the Institute of Notre Dame in Baltimore, a private, all-girls Catholic school. As a Notre Dame student, she was required to wear a uniform—a plaid skirt and a knee-length navy-blue blazer. The school was already more than 100 years old by the time Nancy enrolled in the mid-1950s. Each day, her father's driver dropped her off two blocks from the school—she was too embarrassed to be driven to the door by a chauffeur.

SENATOR BARBARA MIKULSKI, A FELLOW ALUM

Barbara Mikulski graduated from the Institute of Notre Dame in 1954, four years before Nancy Pelosi won her degree from the school. Like Pelosi, Mikulski would go on to become an influential political leader in Washington. She won a seat on the Baltimore City Council in 1971. Five years later, she won an election for the U.S. House, and in 1986, won election to the U.S. Senate.

Mikulski grew up in a Polish neighborhood in Baltimore known as Highlandtown. Her parents were hardly members of the Maryland political elite—her father, William, was a baker; her mother, Christine, worked in a grocery store. At the Institute of Notre Dame, Mikulski did not know Nancy D'Alesandro very well, but years later the two political leaders often spoke with each other about their years at the school. Said Mikulski, "I often laugh and say she came in a limousine, I came in a bus, but we all ended up on the same debating team. It really didn't matter whether you were the mayor's daughter or a grocer's daughter or maybe a new immigrant, we were all treated the same."*

After graduating from the Institute of Notre Dame, Mikulski earned a degree from Mount Saint Agnes College in Maryland. After graduating in 1958, she became a social worker, which led her into community activism. In 1965, transportation planners proposed building a 16-lane thoroughfare linking two interstate highways. The new road would have gone through Fells Point, a residential neighborhood in Baltimore. Mikulski became a leader in the opposition to the highway and was eventually successful in scuttling the plans. Her community activism helped launch her career in Baltimore electoral politics.

The Institute of Notre Dame is housed in an imposing, five-story brick building on Aisquith Street. As Nancy and the other students entered the building, they passed a row of

Like Pelosi, Mikulski has helped break through the marble ceiling in Washington. When she ran for the Senate in 1986, only 18 women in American history had ever served in the upper house of Congress. And all but three of them had been appointed to their seats following the deaths of their husbands. What's more, the only three women who had ever been elected to the Senate in their own right were all Republicans—Margaret Chase Smith of Maine, Nancy Landon Kassebaum of Kansas, and Paula Hawkins of Florida. Incredibly, before Mikulski, no Democratic woman had ever been elected to the Senate in her own right. Said Mikulski, who has never married, "Some guy didn't have to die for me to get my job."**

Around Maryland, Mikulski is known as "Senator Barb." She has won re-election in 1992, 1998, and 2004, and is now the senior female senator in Washington. Mikulski has used her status to mentor other women who have joined the Senate.

As for the Institute of Notre Dame, the school continues to provide education to Catholic girls in Baltimore. About 450 girls enroll in the school each year.

---

* Jamie Steihm, "A Look at the Baltimore Roots of the Two Most Powerful Women in Congress," WYPR News, Baltimore, Feb. 18, 2008. Available online at http://www.publicbroadcasting.net/wypr/news.newsmain?action=article&ARTICLE_ID=1228979§ionID=1.

** Eleanor Clift and Tom Brazaitis. *Madam President: Women Blazing the Leadership Trail.* New York: Routledge, 2003, p. 35.

tall stained-glass murals, each symbolizing the values stressed at the school—charity, praise, duty, science, courage, kindness, faith, art, and prayer. The Catholic sisters who taught Nancy and her classmates encouraged them to become comfortable speaking in public and aspire to leadership roles. Each day, the sisters would post words of inspiration on the school's bulletin board. "The words were the first things you saw when you came into the building back then," Pelosi said. "I still remember them: 'School is not a prison. School is not a playground. It is a time and opportunity.' "[3]

At the Institute, Nancy was a member of the school debate team and volunteered on Saturdays to work in a soup kitchen. In 1957, Nancy's father was invited to attend a dinner at the Emerson Hotel in Baltimore, where a senator from Massachusetts, John F. Kennedy, was being honored for his book, *Profiles in Courage*. When the mayor offered to take Nancy and some friends to the dinner, she jumped at the chance to meet the young senator, who was already being talked about as a possible presidential candidate. Nancy's friend Sally German recalled, "We were high school students and John F. Kennedy sat at the table with us and we talked about his book and it was just astounding—we were mesmerized. Nancy . . . was very composed. She wasn't starstruck, but she admired him a lot."[4] Three years later, Kennedy was elected president. Nancy volunteered in his campaign and attended Kennedy's inaugural ceremony in Washington, D.C.

By then, she was a student at Trinity College, a small women's school in Washington. Her father wanted her to go to college close to home, but Nancy was eager to get out on her own. As a compromise, Tommy and Annunciata permitted her to enroll in a college in Washington, just 35 miles (56 kilometers) from Baltimore. She majored in political science and joined the French Club, Dramatic Society, Political Affairs Club, and International Relations Club. She also helped organize Democratic Party events on campus.

Nancy Pelosi and Senator Barbara Mikulski of Maryland *(right)* joined other Democratic members of Congress at a rally on Capitol Hill in May 2005. Among the others in attendance were *(from left)* Senator Harry Reid of Nevada, Representative Steny Hoyer of Maryland, and Representative Charles Rangel of New York.

One summer, she took a class in African history at nearby Georgetown University. One of her classmates was Paul Pelosi, a student from San Francisco, California. Paul and Nancy started to date. They both graduated in 1962 and were married a year later.

STAY-AT-HOME MOM

They moved first to New York City, where Paul Pelosi intended to pursue a career in investment banking. The couple started to raise a family—four children were born to the Pelosis in their New York home: Nancy Corrine, Christine, Jacqueline, and Paul. A fifth child, Alexandra, was born soon after the Pelosis moved to San Francisco in 1969.

Paul had been drawn back to San Francisco because of the growing computer industry in Northern California, particularly in the region near Stanford University known as Silicon Valley. Few businesses used computers then, and few people understood their potential. Paul joined a company that leased computers to businesses. The Pelosis were able to ride the computer industry as it exploded and, today, they are believed to be worth $50 million or more.

As for Nancy, she worked as a full-time mother. She organized her house with the same fervor and efficiency that her father used to organize his campaigns in Baltimore. All the children were assigned chores at home. Every evening, everybody pitched in to wash the dishes and clean up the kitchen after dinner. Each morning, Nancy supervised the preparation of lunches for school—slices of whole-wheat bread, lunch meats, snacks and apples were all laid out on the kitchen counter, where they were prepared for lunch assembly-line style. During the day, she carpooled with other moms, driving the kids to soccer practice, class trips, and other activities. She brought cupcakes to school for the annual bake sale and sewed the kids' Halloween costumes, including an elaborate pink angel's costume, complete with silver wings, for Alexandra. "My mom was a stay-at-home mom," Alexandra Pelosi recalled. "She made Halloween costumes, and had birthday parties, and drove carpool."[5]

She did find time to keep a hand in local politics, though, helping San Francisco candidates in their campaigns. Just as Nancy and her brothers worked in their father's campaigns, Nancy enlisted the Pelosi children for San Francisco political activities. In the Pelosi home in the city's fashionable Presidio Terrace neighborhood, the kitchen table became campaign headquarters: It was not unusual for the children to come home from school and find stacks of campaign literature and bumper stickers waiting for them. Everybody pitched in, folding literature, stuffing the flyers into envelopes, and then licking the envelopes shut. Said Alexandra, "She modeled our house in San Francisco after the house where she grew up in Baltimore. Our house was like a Veterans of Foreign Wars hall. She'd be working the issues from there, stuffing mailers, having parties."[6]

Indeed, Pelosi proved her value as a fund-raiser to Democratic political leaders in Northern California. Thanks in large part to the connections Paul Pelosi had made in business, the Pelosis were able to attract many large donors to Democratic candidates in San Francisco. In politics, money is often a vital component of a successful campaign. Even races for minor positions require money for printing, postage, and other necessities. Races for seats in Congress and other important offices take enormous amounts of money to buy advertising on television and the radio, to conduct polling, and to pay professional campaign staff members and consultants. San Francisco political leaders were very aware that, if Nancy Pelosi agreed to host a cocktail party or a dinner for a candidate, the dollars would soon flow into that candidate's coffers.

MARYLAND ROOTS

One San Francisco political leader who was particularly close to the Pelosis was Edmund G. Brown Jr., who was known more familiarly as Jerry Brown. Brown's father, Edmund G. "Pat" Brown, had been the governor of California. Paul Pelosi first met Jerry Brown at St. Ignatius High School in San Francisco, where the two were friends and classmates. At first, Jerry Brown harbored no political ambitions—after high school, he studied for the priesthood but then changed his mind and enrolled in the University of California and then Yale Law School. In 1969, the year Paul and Nancy

Pelosi moved to San Francisco, Jerry Brown launched his first political campaign—he won a minor seat on the board of trustees for a local community college. A year later, he ran for a much more substantial seat—secretary of state for California. (Unlike the U.S. secretary of state, who oversees diplomatic relationships with other countries, the secretary of state for a state government typically administers elections and performs many other bureaucratic functions, such as providing licenses for businesses and maintaining the state's official records.) Brown won the election, and soon started to look toward even higher office. In 1974, he was elected governor of California. Two years later, he launched a campaign for the presidency.

Brown found himself in a crowded field. In the wake of the Watergate scandal, more than a dozen Democratic candidates surfaced to seek the White House in 1976. The scandal incriminated aides to Republican President Richard M. Nixon, who were found to have planted illegal electronic listening devices in Democratic Party headquarters at the Watergate hotel and office complex in Washington, D.C. As Nixon tried to cover up their activities, he was drawn more and more into the scandal. Finally facing impeachment in 1974, Nixon resigned. By 1976, Republican politicians were still suffering fallout from the scandal, as Nixon's successor, President Gerald R. Ford, found it hard to put Watergate behind him. His popularity also suffered from a weak economy.

Among the Democrats, the leading contender was Jimmy Carter, the former governor of Georgia who scored an impressive series of wins in the early Democratic primaries of 1976. Indeed, by early May, Carter had won 10 of 13 primaries. By then, Brown, who entered the presidential race late in the spring, had managed to score only a distant second-place finish to Carter in Georgia.

Brown knew that, if he wanted to stop Carter's momentum, he would need a significant victory in a major state.

And so he targeted the May 18 primary in Maryland. To help organize his campaign in Maryland, Brown appealed to Nancy Pelosi. He asked her to return to Maryland to head his campaign in the state and reach out to the political leaders she had known growing up as the daughter of Baltimore Mayor Tommy D'Alesandro. Pelosi agreed to take over the campaign. She said, "That's the episode that took me out of the kitchen and put me into official party responsibilities."[7]

Pelosi got right to work, organizing the Brown campaign in Baltimore and elsewhere in the state just as her father would have organized one of his campaigns: She recruited dozens of volunteers, raised money, knocked on doors, and made phone calls.

Indeed, one of the first phone calls Pelosi made after arriving in Baltimore was to the governor of Maryland, Marvin Mandel. By calling Mandel, Pelosi had reached into her father's favor file. Twenty-four years earlier, Mandel had been a young Democrat climbing the ladder of Maryland politics. In 1952, the mayor of Baltimore, Tommy D'Alesandro, backed Mandel for a vacancy in the state legislature. Mandel won the job and, therefore, owed his career to the D'Alesandro family. Before Pelosi's call, Mandel had been supporting another candidate, Senator Henry Jackson of Washington. After speaking with Pelosi, he quickly changed allegiances.

On April 28, 1976, Jerry Brown arrived in Baltimore to open his campaign for the Maryland presidential primary. He was met at the airport by Governor Mandel, who pledged to support Brown in the election. Mandel immediately tapped the vast resources of the Maryland Democratic Party, providing volunteers, money, and other support to Brown's campaign.

Meanwhile, Carter arrived in Maryland as the clear front-runner for the nomination. Newspaper polls showed him well ahead of Brown and a handful of other rivals who were still in the race. In fact, by late April, polls showed that Brown had the support of just 7 percent of Maryland voters. Still, as the campaign edged closer to Election Day, the gap started to close. Indeed, just a few days before the election, the polls indicated that Carter's lead over Brown had slipped to a razor-thin margin of three points.

Finally, on Election Day, Brown shocked Carter by defeating him with 49 percent of the Democratic vote while the former Georgia governor polled 37 percent, with the other candidates splitting the remaining votes. In reporting on the election, *New York Times* politics writer Ben A. Franklin wrote:

> Governor Brown's seemingly spontaneous Presidential campaign here became an organized stop-Carter drive two weeks ago when Governor Mandel quietly passed the word to his lifelong political allies in Baltimore to get out an anti-Carter vote for Mr. Brown.[8]

COMMITMENT TO DEMOCRATIC CAUSES

Brown won just two more primaries that year, Nevada and his home state of California. After the loss in Maryland, Carter's campaign recovered. He easily won the nomination and, that fall, the general election. Carter's presidency would last just one term, in which the country found itself mired in a deep economic recession while radical Islamic leaders in Iran humiliated the United States in 1979 by storming the American embassy in Tehran and taking 52 embassy workers hostage for more than a year. As events unfolded, voters turned hostile to Carter. In the 1980 election, Brown again ran against Carter for the Democratic nomination, but his campaign fell short. He won just one

California Governor Edmund G. "Jerry" Brown Jr. thanked his supporters at his Baltimore campaign headquarters after he defeated Jimmy Carter in Maryland's Democratic presidential primary in 1976. Nancy Pelosi ran Brown's campaign in Maryland. After Brown's victory, Pelosi's talents as a political organizer and fund-raiser were more and more in demand.

primary—in Michigan. That fall, Carter was defeated for re-election by Ronald Reagan, a former governor of California.

As for Pelosi, after engineering Brown's win in Maryland, she returned to California to find her talents as a political organizer and fund-raiser even more in demand. She became active in the California State Democratic Committee, the statewide organization that oversees all Democratic campaigns. She was soon elected chairwoman of the state organization and used her influence to persuade national Democratic leaders to stage the party's 1984 national convention in San Francisco.

She also became a close friend and ally of Phillip Burton, the member of Congress who had represented San Francisco and nearby portions of Northern California in Washington since 1964. When Burton died in 1983, a special election was held to fill his seat. That election was won by Burton's widow, Sala, who was re-elected in 1984 and 1986. But in 1987, Sala Burton learned that she had cancer. When doctors assured her that she did not have long to live, Burton summoned her friend Nancy Pelosi and urged her to run for her seat. Recalled Sala's brother-in-law John Burton, "They told me Sala wanted Nancy to run for her seat. . . . I thought Sala would say she wanted Nancy because of friendship, but she talked about Nancy's talent and commitment to Democratic causes."[9]

Sala Burton died on Feb. 1, 1987. Two weeks later, state officials scheduled the special election to fill Burton's seat for April 7. Pelosi had roughly seven weeks to put a campaign together.

Rise to the Top

In 1977, the disco group Village People scored its first hit with the song "San Francisco (You've Got Me)." The song praised the city for its liberal attitude and openness. Indeed, these lyrics from the song summed up San Francisco's respect for civil liberties: "Dress the way you please and put your mind at ease . . . It's a city known for its freedom, freedom."[1]

The two members of Congress who had represented the city since 1964—Phillip and Sala Burton—took their city's attitude very seriously as they served in Washington. Phillip Burton served in Congress during the Vietnam War, a conflict he opposed every day he was in office. He was also one of the first members of Congress to recognize the growing threat of Acquired Immune Deficiency Syndrome, the sexually transmitted disease that can often be fatal, and he sponsored legislation to provide federal money for AIDS research and prevention programs. After Phillip's death, Sala continued to champion her husband's causes in Congress, advocating for poor people, education, and the environment, and calling for reductions in military spending.

Clearly, the member of Congress elected to succeed the Burtons would have to reflect the city's respect for personal freedoms and dedication to liberal causes. Shortly after Sala Burton's death, 14 candidates announced their intentions to seek her seat in Congress. Most of them were fringe candidates with little support or chances to win. It became clear that the election would come down to a race between Nancy Pelosi and San Francisco Supervisor Harry Britt.

While Pelosi was ready to carry on the Burtons' liberal tradition on Capitol Hill, most of her work in Democratic politics had been as a behind-the-scenes player: organizing campaigns, raising money, and running political committees. Few people outside a small circle of Northern California political leaders had ever heard of her. Britt, on the other hand, was a veteran San Francisco politician with a long record of achievement on the city's Board of Supervisors. What's more, he was gay. In liberal San Francisco—home to the largest gay population in America—being gay was often a political asset. Gay citizens of San Francisco—who made up an estimated 15 percent of the city's population—were eager to send a gay American to Washington. They planned to rally behind Britt, giving him their overwhelming support in the election.

ROUGH-AND-TUMBLE ELECTION

Pelosi, Britt, and the other candidates had seven weeks to campaign. It turned out to be a rough-and-tumble affair, with Pelosi and Britt exchanging many caustic charges.

During the campaign, Britt acknowledged hiring private detectives to look into Paul Pelosi's business affairs, hoping to uncover improprieties he could use against Nancy in the election. After a thorough investigation, Britt's detectives turned up no evidence of wrongdoing.

For her part, Pelosi decided to take the campaign to Britt. She spent a lot of time that spring in the city's Castro neighborhood, where many gay people made their homes. In speaking to the gay citizens, she promised to defend their rights in Washington, but she also talked about other issues that all people would find important: economic issues, military spending, and environmental protection. As a result, Britt found his support among gays slipping. A month before the election, San Francisco gay-rights leader Kim Corsaro, editor of the publication *Coming Up!*, endorsed Pelosi in the race. Charlie Howell, Pelosi's gay and lesbian issues coordinator, said, "Nancy is fully aware of the issues that the district is concerned about, and you will be hearing a lot about those issues from Washington."[2]

Britt could also not match Pelosi's ability to raise money and organize a campaign. Recalled Pelosi, "We had 100 house parties, and we got 4,000 volunteers to go door to door and to staff phone banks. I raised $1 million in seven weeks."[3]

As Election Day neared, the polls showed Pelosi leading in a tight race. Under California's election laws, the winner would need at least 50 percent of the votes cast to claim the seat. If the top vote-getter received fewer than 50 percent, the race would go to a runoff election, in which the top Democratic finisher would face the top Republican candidate. On the eve of the April 7 election, Britt boldly predicted he would beat Pelosi, citing the overwhelming support he believed he would receive from the gay community. "I expect to get 80 percent of the gay vote,"[4] Britt boasted.

Nancy Pelosi awaited the results of the April 1987 special election to fill the seat of U.S. Representative Sala Burton, who had died in February. Pelosi's biggest competition was Harry Britt, who served on the San Francisco Board of Supervisors.

His prediction would fall short. Britt received a majority of the gay votes, but polls indicated that just 69 percent of gays supported him for the seat, with Pelosi picking up most of the rest. As for the final outcome, Pelosi led the field, garnering about 38,000 votes. Britt finished second, about 4,000 votes behind.

The race, though, was not yet over. Pelosi garnered about 36 percent of the vote, meaning that she faced a runoff election, which was scheduled for June. Her opponent was Harriet Ross, a San Francisco lawyer and the top Republican vote-getter in the April 7 special election. The runoff campaign proved to be just a footnote to the Pelosi-Britt race. In San Francisco, Democrats make up about 65 percent of the city's voter registration rolls, giving few opportunities to Republicans to win elections. In the runoff election on June 2, Pelosi outpolled Ross by a three-to-one margin.

A week later, Pelosi was sworn in to office as the newest member of the U.S. House of Representatives.

SAN FRANCISCO LIBERAL

Once she arrived in Washington, Pelosi intended to follow the liberal course set by the Burtons. She also intended to fulfill the promises she had made to the gay community, representing their interests on Capitol Hill. She became a stalwart proponent for committing federal dollars to programs that addressed the AIDS epidemic. Indeed, throughout the 1980s, the administration of President Ronald Reagan had been slow to respond to the AIDS crisis. Today, because of the effectiveness of drugs, the symptoms of AIDS can largely be controlled, but in the 1980s the disease was almost always fatal and mainly found in gay men. In 1987, the year Pelosi joined Congress, the disease had been responsible for more than 40,000 deaths since it had been first identified six years earlier.

Under Reagan, the federal government had taken virtually no action to stem the rise of the disease until 1986, when Surgeon General C. Everett Koop endorsed the use of condoms to prevent the spread of AIDS. Pelosi lobbied members of the House to commit federal resources to AIDS programs. She helped create the Housing Opportunities for Persons with AIDS program, which provides federal housing assistance for people with AIDS and their families. Pelosi felt the assistance was vital to AIDS patients because they are often too ill to work, which is likely to affect their ability to pay rent or meet other daily expenses. By 2008, the program had provided some $2.3 billion in assistance to nearly 75,000 AIDS patients. "The thing she came here to

LIBERALS AND CONSERVATIVES

The terms "liberal" and "conservative" are often used to describe American politicians. The original description of a conservative is attributed to Edmund Burke, the eighteenth-century British philosopher who argued that political stability is dependent on the careful control of change. Conservatives are, therefore, suspicious of new ideas and prefer that change be made in small steps. Burke wrote, "It is with infinite caution that any man ought to venture upon pulling down an edifice which has answered in any tolerable degree for ages the common purposes of society."* Modern American conservatives generally oppose government intervention in people's lives.

The original description of a liberal was first applied to the anti-royalty activists of England and France in the seventeenth and eighteenth centuries. Calling for democracy, liberal activists hoped to wrest control of their governments from kings whose families held power for generations. These liberals wanted to enact radical change by placing control of the government in the hands of the people. The seventeenth-century English philosopher John Locke is regarded as one of the most influential advocates for liberalism. His essays on liberal thought inspired many advocates for democracy, including James Madison, Thomas Jefferson, and Alexander Hamilton.

Generally, modern liberal politicians believe government should be a major influence in the lives of people. Perhaps the most significant liberal politician of the last 100 years is do was to fight the AIDS epidemic," said Judy Lemons, one of Pelosi's aides on Capitol Hill. "That was the thing that came out from Day 1 for her."[5]

President Franklin D. Roosevelt. In the 1930s, to rescue the country from the Great Depression, Roosevelt established numerous government programs to generate jobs and otherwise provide financial assistance to needy people.

In American politics, Republicans generally regard themselves as conservative thinkers, but few Democrats admit to being liberals. For much of the 1960s and 1970s, the Democratic Party was headed by a number of liberal political leaders, but in the 1980 presidential election, conservative Republican Ronald Reagan was elected in a landslide. Reagan's election sent a message to the leadership of the Democratic Party that it had fallen out of step with mainstream American thinking. Since then, Democrats have tried to steer a path closer to the center of American political thought.

There are, of course, many pockets of liberalism remaining in American society. In 2007, Americans for Democratic Action, a liberal advocacy group that rates members of Congress on their commitments to liberalism, gave 53 members of the House, all Democrats, 100 percent scores for supporting a liberal agenda. Three members of the Senate received perfect scores from the ADA. The ADA did not provide a score for Nancy Pelosi in 2007, since she was speaker of the House; however, in 2006 she received a 95 percent score from the organization.

---

* William Safire, *Safire's Political Dictionary*. New York: Random House, 1992, p. 144.

On Capitol Hill, conservatives who opposed Pelosi's support for gay rights and AIDS programs called her a "San Francisco liberal" and claimed that most Americans did not share her values. But Pelosi countered, "When people say 'San Francisco liberal,' are they talking about protecting the environment, educating the American children, building economic success? No, they are talking about gay people. Well, I believe all people are God's children. And the last time I checked, that included gay people."[6]

IRRITATING THE CONSERVATIVES

Throughout the 1980s and 1990s, Pelosi embraced other positions that irritated conservatives. During the 1990s, conservative leaders in Washington tried to kill the National Endowment for the Arts, the federal agency that subsidizes the work of artists and performers. Conservative politicians had long opposed the NEA, arguing that taxpayers should not have to subsidize the creative arts. Also, many conservatives have bristled at some of the projects the NEA has supported, finding them obscene or in poor taste. In 1997, the House voted to deny funding to the NEA, but the plan died in the Senate. Following the Senate vote, Pelosi worked hard to maintain funding for the NEA—in 2008, the agency received $144.7 million from the federal budget.

Pelosi has argued that spending on the arts is not a frivolous use of public money and that it is important for young people to develop their talents as artists and performers. "Arts education is not just a frill tacked on to the vital work of learning reading, writing, and arithmetic," she said. "Art education increases skills in all these subjects, as well as in language development and . . . reasoning."[7] What's more, in 2002, she authored legislation creating the Challenge America program, which provides grants to obscure artists and performers, many based in small towns, who otherwise would not have qualified for NEA grants.

Since its establishment in 1965, the NEA has provided some $3 billion in grants to artists and performers.

In other votes, Pelosi has opposed permitting prayers in public schools, which is advocated by conservative Christian leaders. She has opposed school vouchers, which would provide parents with taxpayer assistance to send their children to private schools. Conservatives believe voucher programs would force public schools to improve because they would risk losing their students to private schools, but opponents of vouchers contend that they would primarily benefit wealthy Americans whose children comprise a majority of private school enrollments.

Pelosi has long lobbied for laws that would help control guns in America. Conservatives are usually steadfast in their opposition to gun control, arguing that Americans have the right to bear arms under the Second Amendment to the U.S. Constitution. In 1981, though, President Ronald Reagan's press secretary, James Brady, was shot in the head by a mentally ill man who tried to kill the president. Following his recovery, Brady and his wife, Sarah, became advocates for gun-control legislation. Their cause was adopted on Capitol Hill by Pelosi and other gun-control advocates, who sponsored the Brady Bill, requiring extensive background checks on individuals who buy handguns. Conservative politicians fought hard against the law, but in 1993 advocates of gun control finally mustered enough votes for its adoption, and it was signed into law by President Bill Clinton.

ADVOCATING ABORTION RIGHTS

Pelosi favors abortion rights, opposing the law passed by Congress in 2003 that prohibits doctors from performing a late-term abortion procedure known as intact dilation and extraction, or D&X. In most cases, doctors performed the procedure when it appeared that the child would be born with a horrific medical condition. According to the Alan Guttmacher Institute, which studies trends in sexual and reproductive issues, just 2,200 of the 1.3 million abortions performed in the United States in 2000 were through the D&X procedure. Abortion opponents, who call the procedure "partial-birth abortion," regard D&X as barbaric and argue that many women who would give birth to otherwise healthy babies would seek the procedure because they had changed their minds about going through with the births at late stages in their pregnancies. After the law was passed in 2003, its implementation was delayed until 2007 when the U.S. Supreme Court ruled the measure constitutional.

Pelosi's support for abortion rights has often clashed with positions taken by Catholic leaders. Indeed, in 1990, John Cardinal O'Connor of New York suggested that Catholic political leaders who support abortion rights risked excommunication from the church. Pelosi and other pro-choice Catholic politicians, though, stood their ground. "There is no desire to fight with the cardinals or archbishops," she said. "But it has to be clear that we are elected officials, and we uphold the law and we support public positions separate and apart from our Catholic faith."[8]

PROTEST IN TIANANMEN SQUARE

Two years after Pelosi entered Congress, a dramatic and riveting story unfolded across the Pacific Ocean. In Beijing, China, 100,000 students and other pro-democracy advocates gathered in Tiananmen Square to protest the repressive communist regime. After a two-month standoff, Chinese troops moved into the square to break up the demonstration. It is believed that hundreds of protesters were killed in the melee while thousands were arrested.

The brutal crackdown horrified Pelosi. San Francisco is the home of more than 150,000 Chinese Americans, making it one of the largest concentrations of the ethnic group in the United States. As their representative in Congress, Pelosi believed it was her responsibility to make a statement about human-rights abuses in China.

Her opportunity came in 1991. That year, Pelosi and other members of Congress traveled to China. The Chinese government closely monitored the trip. Each day, government officials accompanied the members on their tour of Beijing. One night, however, Pelosi and other representatives slipped out of their hotel and made their way to Tiananmen Square, where they unfurled a banner that read, "To Those Who Died for Democracy in China." To publicize their protest, the lawmakers invited news reporters to accompany them to the square.

Suddenly, the police moved in. They demanded that the Americans turn over the banner. There was some pushing and shoving. "I started running," Pelosi said, "and my colleagues, some of them, got a little roughed up. The press got treated worse because they had cameras, and they were detained."[9] Still, the little demonstration served its purpose. The next day, photographs of Pelosi and the other members holding aloft the banner were published on the front pages of newspapers across the globe.

YEAR OF THE WOMAN

In 1991, President George H.W. Bush nominated Clarence Thomas for a seat on the U.S. Supreme Court. Under law, Supreme Court nominees must be confirmed in a Senate vote. The Thomas nomination appeared to be cruising toward an easy confirmation when Anita Hill, a law professor at the University of Oklahoma, stepped forward with a startling allegation: A decade before, while working as an aide to Thomas, Hill maintained that Thomas had sexually harassed her.

Women in Congress rallied behind Hill. On October 8, in an unprecedented action, seven female members of the House walked to the Senate side of the Capitol, where they demanded an audience with Senate Majority Leader George Mitchell. By then, the Senate had concluded its hearings into Thomas's confirmation and was preparing to vote on the nomination. Mitchell met with the House members and reluctantly agreed to reopen the confirmation hearings. Three days later, Hill had the opportunity to tell her story.

Her testimony riveted the nation, particularly millions of women, who watched the televised hearings at home. Thomas denied the allegations. On October 16, the Senate voted, confirming Thomas for a seat on the court by a razor-thin 52-to-48 margin.

Thomas may have won his seat on the nation's highest court, but a year later women would have their say. In the 1992 elections, which were dubbed the "Year of the Woman" by the media, voters elected 24 new female members of the House and five new female members to the Senate. Women would continue to make gains. In 1987, the year Pelosi joined the House, she was one of 22 female members. By 1998, the number of women in the House had grown to 40. That year, she started to ask colleagues in the Democratic caucus if they would support her for the job of Democratic whip. The feedback was positive, and Pelosi started to campaign for the post. As whip, Pelosi would be charged with counting heads, making deals on the floor, and otherwise corralling caucus members to line up their support on key issues.

Pelosi thought the position might open up in 2000. If the Democrats won back control of the House that year, the minority leader, Richard Gephardt, would become speaker,

Three U.S. lawmakers—*(from left)* Ben Jones of Georgia, Nancy Pelosi, and John Miller of Washington state—unfurled a banner in Tiananmen Square in September 1991 to honor the activists killed during China's pro-democracy protests two years earlier. The Chinese police quickly brought an end to the legislators' demonstration.

and the incumbent whip, David Bonior of Michigan, would become majority leader. The Democrats, though, did not take over the House in 2000, and the race for whip was on hold. A year later, Bonior announced he was stepping down as whip to run for governor of Michigan, so now his position would be open.

For months, Pelosi campaigned for the post as though the election were conducted on the streets of Baltimore. By then, she had been in Congress for more than 14 years. During that time, she had built up allegiances with other members, providing them with key votes on legislation and helping them raise funds for their re-election campaigns. Indeed, she had compiled an impressive favor file of her own and now, as she campaigned for whip, she started to collect from the Democratic caucus members who owed her favors in return. Said Lemons, "We had a huge operation for getting members there, not missing any votes. We had walkie-talkies for tracking every member. That's the total Nancy Pelosi style. Details, details, details. Don't leave anything undone."[10]

Pelosi's opponent, Representative Steny Hoyer of Maryland, campaigned hard as well, but he could not match Pelosi's verve. When the votes were counted, in October 2001, Pelosi tallied 118 votes to 95 for Hoyer. Pelosi was

IN HER OWN WORDS

Nancy Pelosi has continued to push China on human-rights concerns. As China prepared to host the 2008 Summer Olympics, the communist country fell under harsh criticism from human-rights activists for its occupation of Tibet, the mountainous region that has been dominated by the Chinese since 1950. In March 2008, Pelosi visited the Dalai Lama, the exiled spiritual leader of the Tibetan people, at his home in Dharamsala, India, and pledged her support for human rights for the Tibetan people. She also called on President George W. Bush to boycott the opening ceremonies of the Summer Olympics, but Bush refused. Speaking on the House floor, Pelosi said:

> The Tibetan people have accumulated legitimate grievances from six decades of repressive Chinese government policies. They have been economically marginalized in their own land, imprisoned for peacefully

now the first woman to move into the ranks of congressional leadership.

As Democratic whip, Pelosi was second in command in the Democratic caucus behind Richard Gephardt, who had served as minority leader since 1995. Under Gephardt, the Democrats were never able to recapture the majority in the House. In 2002, Gephardt resigned as minority leader, and was succeeded by Pelosi. She had now risen to the top of her caucus and, following the 2006 elections, she would take her place as the first woman speaker of the House. "We made history," Pelosi said, "now we have to make progress."[11]

expressing their views, and barred from practicing their religion independently of government officials.

So powerful is the image of the Dalai Lama that Tibetans are imprisoned for even owning pictures of him. The more Beijing tightens its grip, the more the hearts and minds of the Tibetan people will slip through its fingers ...

During our visit to Dharamsala, we had the opportunity to hear firsthand accounts of beatings, electroshock, and other grotesque techniques Chinese authorities use to punish political prisoners.

Freeing political prisoners in China and Tibet has been a priority for me throughout my congressional career. The stories about the conditions inside the Chinese labor prisons are very familiar. These heroes who are thrown in prison have the courage to speak out for freedom and the determination to withstand years of imprisonment and unspeakable horrors.

The Hundred Hours Agenda

Soon after her election as speaker, Nancy Pelosi announced a legislative agenda for the first 100 hours of her tenure as leader of the House. The so-called Hundred Hours agenda included some bold initiatives that had been blocked by the former Republican leadership of the House as well as the Bush administration—such as funding embryonic stem cell research, assisting college students with more affordable student loans, and helping elderly citizens by making their prescription drugs more affordable. As Pelosi surveyed the political landscape, though, it was clear that her first job as speaker would be to restore voters' confidence in Congress.

Indeed, the list of scandals that had plagued the House was long and embarrassing. In the two years leading up to the 2006 elections, two members of Congress, Randy Cunningham of California and Robert Ney of Ohio, had been jailed in bribery scandals. The former majority leader, Tom DeLay of Texas, had been indicted on charges of hiding campaign contributions, then using the money to attack his political enemies. Another powerful member, Curt Weldon of Pennsylvania, was under investigation for using his influence to steer business to a company headed by his daughter. Florida House member Mark Foley resigned after reports surfaced that he had made improper sexual advances to the young pages who work on Capitol Hill. And Representative William Jefferson of Louisiana was under investigation, and later indicted, on bribery charges after federal agents found $90,000 stashed in the freezer of his home.

And so on January 4, 2007, her first day as speaker, Pelosi proposed a list of reforms designed to enhance the ethical conduct of House members. The new rules barred members of the House from accepting gifts, meals, or trips from lobbyists or the special-interest groups that hire them. The House passed Pelosi's recommendations by an overwhelming margin, voting 430 to 1 to adopt the new rules for ethical conduct. Pelosi, however, believed further reforms were necessary. She established a task force composed of lawmakers to determine whether the House Ethics Committee should be replaced by a much more effective watchdog panel.

The Ethics Committee, made up of members of the House, had been established to investigate ethics abuses among members. Clearly, the committee had been ineffective—it did not start a probe of Cunningham's activities until *after* the California congressman had resigned and gone to prison. Pelosi had hoped the task force could recommend reforms within a few months, but the process dragged on for more than a year. Finally, in early 2008, the task force recommended establishment of the independent Office of Congressional Ethics, to be administered by a six-member board. Under the rules proposed by the task force, the speaker and the minority leader would each name three members to the board; none of the board members would be members of Congress. In other words, for the first time an independent group of outsiders would be charged with policing the ethical conduct of House members. Pelosi believed that an independent group of watchdogs would be able to operate outside the culture of Capitol Hill, where influential members of Congress could use their power to kill probes into unethical conduct.

The House acted on the task force's recommendations, establishing the Office of Congressional Ethics in March 2008 by a vote of 229 to 182, with mostly Republicans voting against the new panel. Republican leaders complained that the House should take care of its own business. "We don't need a new layer of bureaucracy to stand between those who break the rules and those who must enforce them,"[1] insisted House Minority Leader John Boehner. Pelosi countered, though, that the House had simply never done a very good job of policing the conduct of its own members, and it was time for independent oversight. The new ethics panel, she said, "represents what I believe is necessary for us to convey to the American people what we owe them: our best effort to have this Congress live up to the highest ethical standard."[2]

LONGER WORK WEEK

The ethics reforms were the first achievement in the Hundred Hours agenda that Pelosi laid out for the House on her first day as speaker. By setting a goal of accomplishing the agenda within 100 hours, Pelosi did not intend for the House to work round-the-clock for 100 straight hours, a time span that would cover just a handful of days. Rather, she wanted to see the agenda accomplished within the first 100 hours in which the House was in session, a span of time that could last several weeks.

Under the previous House leadership, members spent very few hours a week actually in session. For years, the House worked only Tuesdays to Thursdays, giving members Mondays, Fridays and weekends away from Capitol Hill to spend with their families, perform services for their constituents, or travel between Washington and their home districts.

Critics complained, though, that just three days a week devoted to legislative business was not enough time for the House to craft meaningful legislation. In fact, the legislative week wasn't even three days. Typically, the House leadership would wait until Tuesday evening to gavel the chamber to order, then adjourn early Thursday afternoon, giving members a head start on their weekends.

After taking over as speaker, Pelosi told members to expect to begin their time on the House floor no later than Monday afternoons and to be prepared to work through Friday evenings. The new schedule caused a considerable amount of grumbling in the ranks. One longtime member, Republican Jack Kingston of Georgia, complained, "Keeping us here eats away at families. Marriages suffer. The Democrats could care less about families—that's what this says."[3] But other members of the House said they were prepared to make the sacrifice. Democrat Debbie Wasserman Schultz of Florida said she would have to find another way to run her 7-year-old daughter's Brownie troop meetings, which had been held on Monday afternoons. "I'll have to talk to the other mothers to see if we can move it to the weekend,"[4] she said.

Another measure that Pelosi introduced after taking office was to ban smoking in the House. Smoking in all other federal buildings had been prohibited since 1997 under an executive order signed by President Bill Clinton. The House had maintained an exemption, though, permitting smoking in the ornate Speaker's Lobby—a place where politicians often huddled together under clouds of cigar smoke. "We can no longer risk the health of colleagues, staff, pages, reporters, and others who pass through the Speaker's Lobby each day,"[5] Pelosi insisted, and within hours the ashtrays in the lobby had been removed.

TAKING ON THE DRUG COMPANIES

With the House now in session five days a week, Pelosi started to push the significant issues on her Hundred Hours agenda. Over the next few weeks, the new speaker would find mixed success. She was able to win adoption of some of her initiatives. In some cases, though, the House passed her agenda, but the measures were eventually killed by the Senate or the White House. (In Washington, for a bill to become a law, it must be passed in both the Senate and the House and signed by the president.)

One of the top items on Pelosi's Hundred Hours agenda was to raise the minimum wage—the salary earned by America's lowest-paid workers. Less than a week after taking office as speaker, Pelosi was able to forge a compromise with the GOP on raising the minimum wage—it was the first time in 10 years that Congress acted to amend the law. Since 1997, the minimum wage had been $5.15 an hour—a paltry sum that provided a full-time wage earner with just a little more than $200 a week, or just over $10,000 a year. Few people are able to survive in the American economy on such a lean salary.

At Pelosi's urging, Congress raised the minimum wage to $5.85 in 2007, $6.55 in 2008, and $7.25 in 2009. The House voted 315 to 116 to adopt the new standards, with most Democrats and several Republicans supporting the measure. "For 10 years, the lowest-paid Americans have been frozen out,"[6] asserted Representative George Miller, a Democrat from California.

On another measure—finding a way to reduce the cost of prescription medications—Pelosi faced much stiffer opposition. Under existing law, the federal health-care program for senior citizens, Medicare, is prohibited from negotiating prices for prescription drugs with drug manufacturers. That is not true in other countries—in Canada, for example, the government does negotiate the price of prescription medications, a circumstance that has resulted in drug prices that are as much as half the cost in Canada as they are in the United States. Because drug prices are so much cheaper in Canada, many elderly Americans, as well as others, buy their prescription drugs off the Internet from Canadian-based pharmacies.

Pelosi and her colleagues proposed a law that would have enabled Medicare to negotiate prices with drug companies. If Congress passed the law, proponents argued that it would lower drug prices paid by some 22 million older Americans. Pelosi and her supporters said the plan could save senior citizens hundreds of millions of dollars a year. "We have never gotten answers as to what the pharmaceutical companies are charging . . . and what Medicare beneficiaries are getting back for it,"[7] contended Representative Pete Stark of California, who supported the legislation.

Opponents countered that private insurers already negotiate drug prices with pharmaceutical companies and that prices would not come down further simply because the federal government joined the negotiations. Nevertheless, the House passed the legislation by an impressive 255-to-170 margin. "Today's vote is a resounding victory for America's seniors over the special interests," Pelosi declared after the votes were counted. "With today's vote, a strong majority in the House stood behind the millions of Americans who are finding it more difficult to make ends meet under the weight of ever costlier prescription drugs."[8]

Pelosi's victory would prove to be short-lived. The House bill was opposed by the drug companies, which feared huge profit losses. Ultimately, the bill died in the Senate after drug-company lobbyists influenced a sufficient number of senators to kill the legislation. Even if the bill had passed the Senate, it would have been vetoed by President George W. Bush, a longtime opponent of government involvement in the private sector.

SUPPORTING STEM CELL RESEARCH

Another measure backed by Pelosi during the Hundred Hours agenda called for the House to authorize federal financial assistance for stem cell research. Under Bush, virtually all federal funds for embryonic stem cell research had been cut off. Although some Republicans backed the research, Bush steadfastly refused to authorize funding.

Stem cells are extracted from embryos discarded at in vitro fertilization clinics. At the clinics, women who are unable to conceive children can often have their eggs fertilized outside their bodies, then returned to their wombs where the fetus develops naturally. Since embryos are left over after the procedure, scientists believe the embryonic stem cells can be harvested and injected into other people, where they can grow into healthy cells. Proponents of stem cell research believe the procedure holds great promise for the eradication of disease because healthy stem cells can replace diseased cells. Opponents, however, argue that the procedure destroys the embryos, which can be frozen and fertilized later. People who have been born through this procedure are known as "snowflake children" because they were conceived from once-frozen embryos.

In the years in which the federal government has refused to fund most stem cell research projects, some state governments and private corporations have underwritten the research.

Although proposed on the House floor as part of the Hundred Hours agenda, debate on funding stem cell research dragged on for months. In fact, the House would not take a full vote on the measure until June 2007. During the debate, Pelosi spoke in favor of the legislation. She said, "Science is a gift of God to all of us, and science has taken us to a place that is biblical in its power to cure. And that is the embryonic stem cell research."[9]

Opponents argued that recent scientific research indicated stem cells could be extracted from adult donors and made to grow into healthy cells in other people's bodies. Therefore, they argued, there was no reason to destroy healthy embryos. Said Pennsylvania Representative Joseph R. Pitts, who opposed embryonic stem cell research, "How many more advancements in noncontroversial, ethical adult stem cell research will it take before Congress decides to catch up with science? These have all of the potential and none of the controversy."[10]

The House voted on June 7 to authorize federal funding of embryonic stem cell research. More than three dozen Republicans joined the Democratic majority in support of the legislation, which passed by a vote of 247 to 176. The Senate had passed the legislation in April, but it was ultimately vetoed by the president. Said Bush, "If this bill would have become law, American taxpayers would, for the first time in our history, be compelled to fund the deliberate destruction of human embryos. And I'm not going to allow it."[11] Back in the House, Pelosi was unable to muster enough votes to override Bush's veto. To override the president's veto, supporters of the legislation would need a two-thirds majority, or 292 votes. The House vote failed, with only 235 members voting to override Bush's veto.

Nancy Pelosi signed legislation to authorize federal funding of embryonic stem cell research during a ceremony on June 7, 2007. Seated with her was Senate Majority Leader Harry Reid. President George W. Bush vetoed the bill, and the House could not muster enough votes to override the president's veto.

MAKING COLLEGE MORE AFFORDABLE

The failure to fund stem cell research represented a defeat for Pelosi, but Bush and the Republicans in Congress did support another Pelosi initiative in which she sought to make college education somewhat more affordable by reducing the interest rates on student loans and by also increasing direct grants to students.

Indeed, college is an extremely expensive proposition for most American students. According to the College Board, the nonprofit organization that represents about 5,400 American colleges and universities, the average annual cost of an education at a private college in 2008 was nearly $24,000, while at a public university, the average cost was more than $6,000.

Many students earn scholarships that pay some of the cost of their educations. Parents often pay a large portion of students' tuitions, but very often students must take out loans to finance some portion of their educations.

Most students qualify for loans that are subsidized by the federal government; in other words, their interest rates are kept low because taxpayers help them pay back the loans. Also, the loans do not have to be paid back until after graduation, when the student would have a job and is able to make the payments. Still, such loans often don't cover the entire cost of tuition and other college costs—including room and board, books, and supplies—and students must often seek additional money from private lenders, such as banks and similar institutions. After graduation, most students find they have to pay off student-loan debts that total $17,500 or more.

For starters, the bill drafted under Pelosi's guidance punished private lenders who had been showering university financial-aid officers with gifts and other incentives for steering students to those companies. Such tactics usually resulted in higher costs for the students, who often did not take advantage of competing loan offers before signing with the lenders promoted by the universities.

To punish the lenders, Congress slashed subsidies to the private institutions by 80 percent over five years. The lenders complained that the interest rates charged to the students—in other words, the cost of borrowing the money—would increase without the federal aid, but Congress compensated by cutting the interest rates on money the federal government lends directly to students. Before adoption of the bill, the interest rate was 6.8 percent; under the new legislation, the rate was reduced over a

IN HER OWN WORDS

When House Speaker Nancy Pelosi urged her colleagues in the House to adopt new measures to help college students pay for their educations, she likened the federal aid program to the G.I. Bill of Rights, the government's program that helps returning veterans pay for college educations. In a speech on the House floor, Pelosi said:

> Over the years, the G.I. Bill has offered opportunity and economic security through education to more than 20 million of the brave men and women who wore our nation's uniform. It has given America hundreds of thousands of engineers, teachers, and doctors. And it has given us a model for the value in investing in the education of our people for our country. ... With this legislation, we will make the single largest increase in college aid since the G.I. Bill of Rights revolutionized America.
>
> It is an investment to a bright future for our children, just as the G.I. Bill had been an investment in a bright future for our nation. Any economist will tell you that any dollar spent on education is a dollar that makes a big return to our Treasury. In fact, no dollar invested or spent, no tax credit, no financial initiative you can name brings more money to the Treasury than investing in education.
>
> In today's competitive job market, a college education often makes all the difference. Americans with college degrees can earn 60 percent more than those with only high school diplomas. So in the interest of individuals, this is very important.
>
> Indeed, higher education is the single best investment our young people can make in themselves, their families can make in them, and our country can make in our future.

five-year period to 3.4 percent. By cutting the interest rate in half, students could potentially save hundreds of dollars a year in payments.

Also, the law increased the amount of money available to students in the form of grants, which is money the students do not have to pay back. Pelosi said, "We will broaden college opportunity, and we will begin by cutting interest rates for students in half."[12]

Pelosi found a lot of support in the House for the measure, which passed by a vote of 356 to 71. The measure also passed the Senate and, that fall, the 2007 College Cost Reduction and Access Act was signed into law by President Bush.

Pelosi's first few weeks in the House saw the adoption of new ethics-reform measures, more affordable student loans, and a higher minimum wage. Also, Congress worked harder, delivering legislation by convening five days a week. On the other hand, Pelosi was unable to push through legislation lowering prescription drug costs for elderly patients or ensuring that embryonic stem cell research would receive federal funding. Nevertheless, the House acted on all the initiatives in Pelosi's Hundred Hours agenda. In fact, most of the legislation went to votes in the House by January 19—just 15 days after she accepted the gavel as speaker. Although some of the legislation eventually died in the Senate or was vetoed by the president, Pelosi felt that the House had accomplished much during her first few weeks as speaker. Indeed, it had taken just 42 legislative hours to vote on most of the bills Pelosi included in the Hundred Hours agenda. Said Pelosi, "It was a way to say that this Congress will no longer be a place where optimism and good ideas come to die."[13]

Thawing the Middle East Ice

After three months as speaker, Nancy Pelosi had clearly earned the respect of her colleagues as well as others in Washington. "She's a deal-maker and a tough party leader,"[1] said Boston University congressional historian Julian Zelizer. Fellow Democrats also had praise for Pelosi, while some Republican leaders showed her a grudging respect. Said Peter King, a Republican member of Congress from Long Island, New York, "She's shown herself to be friendly, engaging, intelligent."[2]

President George W. Bush and other administration officials would soon find reason to disagree. As Pelosi wrapped up her Hundred Hours agenda, she planned a trip to the Middle East, which has long been one of the most volatile regions on the planet. By then, the war in

Iraq had entered its fourth year. What's more, peace negotiations between the Israelis and the Palestinian Authority, the government that oversees the Palestinian territories, had been stalled for months. In Washington, Bush had failed to make a significant initiative toward helping the Israelis and Palestinians reach an agreement. Meanwhile, Bush refused to back down from his commitment to use force to stabilize Iraq.

It is not unusual for members of Congress to travel to other countries on fact-finding missions. In this case, however, Pelosi and six other members of the House (five Democrats and one Republican) elected to include Syria on their itinerary. Syria has long been regarded as a rogue nation that supports terrorism, supplying arms and money to Hamas and Hizbollah, two terrorist organizations committed to the destruction of Israel. The Bush administration has also criticized Syria for allowing arms to enter Iraq over the border it shares with the war-torn country. For years, the United States and Syria have maintained icy relations, which have resulted in no face-to-face talks between diplomats from the two countries. Said Bush, "Sending delegations hasn't worked. It's just simply been counterproductive."[3]

YEARS OF SUSPICION AND ANIMOSITY

Arabs and Jews have harbored suspicions and animosity toward one another since the closing days of World War I, when a series of diplomatic blunders and duplicities virtually ensured decades of hostility in the Middle East. During the war, the British government adopted the Balfour Declaration, supporting establishment of a Jewish homeland in the Middle East. Meanwhile, the British promised the Arabs independence and sovereignty if they fought against the Ottoman Turks. Arab leaders accepted the offer and fought bravely alongside the British during the war. At the conclusion of the war, they expected their sovereignty to extend over the entire Middle East, including the territory west of the Jordan River set aside as the Jewish homeland. Finally, under the Sykes-Picot Agreement, the English and the French secretly agreed to carve up much of the former Ottoman Empire for themselves, keeping vast regions of the Middle East under their control.

Following World War I, the British granted the Arabs limited sovereignty but were slow to relinquish control over the territory west of the Jordan River known as Palestine. Activist Jews agitated for independence, with some turning to guerrilla tactics to drive out the British. World War II interrupted the campaign for Jewish statehood but, following the war, the British finally made good on their promise to the Jews, granting independence to the new country, to be called Israel. On May 14, 1948, the United Nations voted to formally recognize Israel. A day after the U.N. vote, the armies of five Arab states—Egypt, Jordan, Iraq, Syria, and Lebanon—attacked the Israelis, insisting that the territory belonged to the Arabs. The outmanned and ill-equipped Israeli army outfought the Arabs, who, despite their numbers and arms, lacked training, leadership, and the will to fight. The 1948 Arab-Israeli War ended in a humiliating defeat for the Arab states. Perhaps the most unfortunate victims of the fighting were the 600,000 Palestinian Arabs who fled Israel; many of them found homes in the squalid refugee camps of the West Bank, a region between Israel and Jordan that borders the Jordan River.

Israelis and Arabs would continue to skirmish for years. They would also fight two major wars, in 1967 and 1973. Both resulted in Israeli victories, with Israel occupying vast regions of Arab territory—including the West Bank—to serve as buffer zones against future attacks. Following the 1973 war, two Arab states—Egypt and Jordan—signed formal peace treaties with Israel, while the other Arab states have maintained an uneasy cease-fire with Israel. As for the Palestinians, they remain a stateless people. There have been many attempts by leaders of Israel and the Arab states to negotiate terms under which the West Bank can be granted independence, but Israel has refused to remove its troops from the region unless leaders of the Palestinian Authority can offer assurances that the West Bank will not serve as a launching point for further attacks against Israel. Meanwhile, there is much division within the Palestinian leadership. Moderates have sought peace with Israel while hard-line Palestinians, including leaders of the terrorist group Hamas, have advocated destruction of the Jewish state.

SPARKING A DIALOGUE

And so that was the morass that Pelosi and her six colleagues stepped into when they arrived in the Middle East in early April 2007. Besides Syria, the delegation planned to visit Israel, Lebanon, the West Bank, and Saudi Arabia. Bush administration officials bristled over Pelosi's decision to meet with President Bashar Assad of Syria. Robert F. Turner, a former assistant secretary of state, suggested that, in meeting with Assad, Pelosi would be in violation of the Logan Act, a federal law that prohibits anybody except the president, or a representative of the president, from conducting foreign policy. He said, "House Speaker Nancy Pelosi may well have committed a felony in traveling to Damascus this week, against the wishes of the president, to communicate on foreign-policy issues with Syrian President Bashar Assad. . . . She is certainly not the first member of Congress—of either party—to engage in this sort of behavior, but her position as a national leader, the wartime circumstances, the opposition to the trip from the White

House, and the character of the regime she has chosen to approach make her behavior particularly inappropriate."[4]

Vice President Dick Cheney also criticized Pelosi. "This is an evil man," Cheney said of Assad. "He's a prime state sponsor of terror. So for the speaker to go to Damascus and meet with this guy and treat him with the respect and dignity ordinarily accorded the head of a foreign state—we think it is just directly contrary to our national interest."[5]

Pelosi and other members of the delegation planned the trip because they felt that the Bush administration's foreign policy had alienated many U.S. allies in the Middle East and elsewhere. In the months leading up to the 2003 invasion of Iraq, the Bush administration had ignored calls by the United Nations to seek a diplomatic solution to the tensions with Saddam Hussein. As the war dragged on, the administration ignored calls to draw other states into peace negotiations with the warring factions within Iraq. Many foreign-policy experts had suggested that states like Syria and Iran could use their influence in Iraq to defuse hostilities, but the Bush administration had refused to seek their help. In defense of Pelosi, *Philadelphia Inquirer* foreign-affairs columnist Trudy Rubin said, "President Bush still doesn't grasp the meaning of the 2006 elections. The Democrats who took control of Congress were propelled by voters who wanted a change in Iraq policy. Four years of Iraq turmoil exposed the strategic fraud of a policy that relied mainly on military means to remake the region. It underscored the need for the kind of diplomacy this White House has scorned."[6]

As Pelosi and the others arrived in the Middle East, they were well aware of the controversy that brewed at home over their decision to meet with Assad. But they also harbored no delusions about solving the region's many problems. Instead, they simply hoped to spark a dialogue.

During a trip to the Middle East in April 2007, Nancy Pelosi met with President Bashar Assad of Syria. Officials in the Bush administration condemned Pelosi for meeting with Assad, but Pelosi said the United States needed to engage countries like Syria.

"SHADOW PRESIDENCY"

On April 1, the delegation arrived in Jerusalem, where Pelosi and the other members of Congress met with Prime Minister Ehud Olmert of Israel. Pelosi also addressed the Israeli parliament, which is known as the Knesset. Speaker of the Knesset is Dalia Itzik, who is also the first woman to hold the position. "I salute you for your achievements as the Knesset's first woman speaker," Pelosi said in her speech. "I stand with you tonight, conscious of all that you and I owe to the hopes and dreams of generations of Israeli and American women."[7] Pelosi then pledged her support to maintaining Israel's security.

The congressional delegation arrived in the Syrian capital of Damascus on April 3. Before meeting with Assad,

Pelosi and the others visited a bazaar, where they mingled with ordinary Syrians. Many Syrians crowded around the entourage, impressed that the leader of the delegation was a woman—a rarity in a strict Islamic country. Syrians admitted to being charmed by the speaker. Damascus shop owner Izzat Abdoulkarim said, "Ms. Pelosi is going to be very happy in Syria. George Bush says we are bad, but she will see this is not true. She views the world through a different perspective than Bush. She's more open-minded."[8]

The delegation also visited historic sites in the capital, including an ancient Christian tomb and the eighth-century Omayyad Mosque, where Pelosi, wearing customary apparel for an Arabic woman—a head scarf and a long robe—watched Muslim men participate in a religion class.

Finally, Pelosi and the other members of the delegation met with Assad. They spoke frankly with the Syrian leader, pressing him to cease his support for Hamas and Hizbollah. Assad replied that Syria would be open to participating in talks that would lead to an independent Palestinian homeland in the West Bank. Days before, when Pelosi had met with Olmert in Jerusalem, she came to believe that the Israeli prime minister would be willing to open peace negotiations with the Syrians. That is the message she delivered to Assad, who responded that Syria would, in turn, be willing to meet with the Israelis.

While it would seem that Pelosi's diplomacy had opened something of a dialogue between the two feuding nations, that was not the case. The Israelis remain highly suspicious of the Syrians. After Pelosi's meeting with Assad, Olmert's office was quick to release a statement denying the prime minister's willingness to meet with the Syrian president. The Israelis insisted that Syria demonstrate clearly that it would no longer supply arms to Hamas and Hizbollah before they would be willing to open negotiations with Assad. Simply assuring a group of American lawmakers that Assad would cooperate with peace plans is not good enough, Olmert's office said. According to Olmert's office, the prime minister still considered Syria "a party encouraging terrorism in the entire Middle East."[9]

Back in the United States, Pelosi's critics jumped on her diplomatic misstep. *The Washington Post* published a harsh editorial, insisting that "Ms. Pelosi's attempt to establish a shadow presidency is not only counterproductive, it is foolish."[10] Added the newspaper, "As any diplomat with knowledge of the region could have told Ms. Pelosi, Mr. Assad is a corrupt thug whose overriding priority at the moment is not peace with Israel. . . . The really striking development here is the attempt by a Democratic congressional leader to substitute her own foreign policy for that of a sitting Republican president."[11] And former House Speaker Newt Gingrich said, "One wonders what Speaker Pelosi was thinking when she went to Damascus to meet with the Syrian dictator. When the White House asked her not to do it, she would have gained points by cooperating."[12]

Pelosi dismissed the criticism. She pointed out that, during her meeting with Assad, the Syrian president also promised to provide more stability along Syria's border with Iraq to help stop insurgents from smuggling weapons into the country for use against the American military. Following the meeting, Pelosi said, "We came in friendship, hope, and determined that the road to Damascus is a road to peace."[13]

CHARMING THE SAUDIS

Pelosi made one stop in the Middle East designed to show that she was wary of Syria's intentions. The delegation stopped briefly in Lebanon, a country torn by civil war for much of the 1970s and 1980s. Syrian troops finally moved in to maintain peace, but in 2005 Assad withdrew his troops following the assassination of Lebanese Prime Minister

Rafik Hariri. Hariri had been steering the country away from Syrian domination and feuded with Assad. A team of United Nations investigators has been established to probe the murder of Hariri, which was carried out by a suicide bomber. Many Middle East observers suspect that Assad or other anti-Hariri officials in the Syrian government may be implicated in the assassination—charges that the Syrian government has vigorously denied. In the Lebanese capital of Beirut, Pelosi's delegation visited Hariri's grave and called for the U.N. panel to get to the truth in the case.

The delegation also visited the West Bank and met with Palestinian Authority President Mahmoud Abbas. Considered a moderate, Abbas had agreed to meet with Olmert at least twice a month to see if they could ultimately resolve their differences and establish an independent Palestinian state.

Finally, the delegation arrived in Saudi Arabia, where Pelosi found herself in a society where women do not have a chance to rise high in the government. The country is ruled by the descendants of Abd al-Aziz Al Saud, whose family has held power since the 1920s. The current monarch, King Abdullah, rules with almost absolute power. The king, however, has permitted a legislature, the *Majlis al-Shura*, or Consultative Council, to serve in an advisory capacity and to propose new laws. (The king appoints the council's 150 members.) The Saudis practice a particularly conservative form of Islam that does not give women equal rights with men. In Saudi Arabia, selection of a woman to the Consultative Council is prohibited.

Still, as Pelosi met with Abdullah and other Saudi officials, she did raise the issue of female participation in the Consultative Council, although she was careful not to criticize the kingdom for its policy of excluding women from the halls of power. Saudi Arabia is a major supplier of oil to the United States and other Western nations. It is also a staunch ally in the Middle East, providing assistance to the United States in tracking down terrorists.

While visiting the Saudi capital of Riyadh, the delegation was given a tour of the Consultative Council chambers. The speaker of the council, Sheik Saleh bin Humaid, greeted Pelosi by placing his right hand on his chest. Bin Humaid is also an Islamic cleric; under conservative Islamic law, clerics are not permitted to shake hands with women. Pelosi understood the gesture and returned the greeting by placing her hand on her chest.

With the official greetings out of the way, Pelosi was invited by bin Humaid to sit in the speaker's seat. "It's a nice view from here," she said. "This chair is very comfortable."[14] The delegation also met with King Abdullah at his sprawling farm outside the capital. There, Pelosi urged the king to support the Palestinian-Israeli peace negotiations, and the king said he would. A day after meeting with the king, the delegation returned to the United States.

SYRIA TO THE SUMMIT

Pelosi's diplomatic mission to the Middle East may have stirred criticism back home, but months after her return, the Syrians shocked Bush administration officials when they announced their desire to participate in a peace summit in Annapolis, Maryland. The summit was called by Secretary of State Condoleezza Rice to begin negotiations on an Israeli-Palestinian treaty that could lead to Palestinian statehood. In Washington, Bush had made establishment of a permanent Palestinian homeland a priority before he leaves office in January 2009, and he instructed Rice to convene a summit and invite representatives of the Middle East states to attend.

Syria announced it would send its deputy foreign minister—a relatively minor official; nevertheless, the presence of the Syrian diplomat at the summit indicated to American officials that the Syrians might finally be

(continues on page 70)

RECOGNIZING AN ATROCITY

While Nancy Pelosi's visit to Syria may have opened the way for a dialogue between the United States and the Middle East nation, another foreign policy initiative by the speaker found little support, even among Democrats in the House.

In 2007, Pelosi urged adoption of a House resolution condemning the Turkish government for the 1915 Armenian genocide at the hands of the Ottoman Turks, who ruled Turkey at the time. Turkish troops, fearing that the Armenians would aid the Russians during World War I, deported millions of Armenians, most in a long and cruel march that killed some 1.2 million refugees.

It is not unusual for Congress to pass resolutions that take positions on historic events. For example, in 1988, Congress issued a formal apology to the Japanese-American citizens who were interned during World War II under suspicion that they were spies and saboteurs. That resolution eventually led to the federal government issuing $20,000 checks to everyone who had been held in the camps.

In this case, the congressional resolution would be ceremonial only. It would include no measures to penalize modern Turkey for a genocide that occurred nearly a century ago. Still, leaders in Turkey opposed the resolution. Over the years, the Turkish government has never acknowledged the responsibility of the Ottomans for the genocide. What's more, Turkish officials warned that, if Congress passed the resolution, relations between the two countries could become strained.

Turkey is the lone Islamic country that is governed as a true democracy. Also, the country's strategic location makes it important for Americans to remain on good terms with

Turkish leaders. The country is positioned as a link between Eastern Europe and the Middle East; in fact, it shares a border with Iraq and is regarded as a stabilizing force in the region. In addition, the Turks permit the U.S. military to ferry supplies to Iraq through Turkish air space. Turkish officials warned that, if Congress adopted the resolution, they might withdraw that permission, forcing the military to find another way to deliver arms and other supplies to the American troops.

For months, Pelosi stood steadfast in her determination to recognize the genocide of the Armenian people. Pelosi stood behind the resolution largely because California is the home of some 230,000 Armenian Americans, which is more than half the Armenian American population of the United States. Many of those Armenian Americans live in Pelosi's district.

Despite the speaker's influence, the measure fell short. Pressure by the White House, the Turkish government, and other members of Congress eventually killed the resolution. Said Senate Republican Leader Mitch McConnell, "I think it's a really bad idea for Congress to be condemning what happened 100 years ago. We all know it happened. There's a genocide museum, actually, in Armenia to commemorate what happened. But I don't think Congress passing this resolution is a good idea at any point. But particularly not a good idea when Turkey is cooperating with us in many ways, which ensures greater safety for our soldiers."*

---

*"Pelosi Says She'll Press on with Armenian 'Genocide' Resolution." CNN, October 14, 2007. Available online at http://www.cnn.com/2007/POLITICS/10/14/us.turkey/index.html.

Sheik Saleh bin Humaid, the speaker of the Consultative Council in Saudi Arabia, welcomed Nancy Pelosi to the council's chambers. Pelosi carefully raised the issue of participation by women in the Consultative Council, which has no female members.

(continued from page 67)

willing to participate in regional peace efforts. What's more, Syria made the decision to attend the summit even though its longtime ally in the Middle East, Iran, said the summit would be a waste of time. In Israel, political leader Ran Cohen said, "I think Israel has to receive this as a great opportunity, that Syria comes for diplomatic negotiations . . . to prevent the next war, advance us perhaps toward peace, and also to isolate Iran."[15]

In addition, in testimony before Congress in the fall of 2007, General David Petraeus, the American military commander in Iraq, reported that Syria had stepped up patrols of its border with Iraq and that fewer weapons and insurgents were finding their way into the country. Clearly, Pelosi's overtures to Assad had made something of a difference.

Opposing the War

After returning from the Middle East, Nancy Pelosi prepared for what she believed would be her most important mission: ending the war in Iraq. There is no question that the single most important issue that propelled the Democrats into power in the 2006 election was the public's weariness of the war; once taking control of Congress, Democratic leaders insisted that the war be moved to the top of the legislative agenda.

Shortly after the 2003 invasion, as American troops easily swept aside the Iraqi defenders, support for the war in the United States was overwhelming and President George W. Bush's popularity was at its peak. But those early months of jubilation soon turned into dread, as it became clear that the Bush administration failed to define a clear post-invasion strategy. Soon, heavy fighting broke out among radical militias dominated by Sunnis and Shiites, followers of two different paths of Islam who for centuries have harbored suspicions and ill will toward one another. What's more, the terrorist group al-Qaeda exerted itself in Iraq. Meanwhile, in 2004, news organizations reported abuse of Iraqi prisoners at the Abu Ghraib military prison. Critics suggested the abuse of the Abu Ghraib prisoners might have violated the Geneva Conventions, the international treaty that governs the treatment of prisoners of war. When the Abu Ghraib charges aired, many Americans questioned their country's role in the conflict. Also in 2004, a young American, Nicholas Berg, was kidnapped in Iraq and then brutally executed by terrorists, sparking calls by Americans for the president to find a way out of the morass.

In the months leading up to the 2006 election, Pelosi and other Democratic leaders called for the president to dismiss Secretary of Defense Donald H. Rumsfeld, the chief architect of the administration's flawed war strategy. Said Pelosi, "Secretary Rumsfeld's leadership of the Pentagon has unnecessarily jeopardized the safety of American troops, and it has seriously undermined our ability to prosecute the war on terrorism. The Pentagon Secretary Rumsfeld oversees has become an island of unaccountability, ignoring the Geneva Conventions, our allies, and common sense."[1]

For months, Bush stood steadfast against Pelosi and his other critics, refusing to fire Rumsfeld. But on the day after the 2006 elections, Pelosi called reporters into her office and again demanded that Rumsfeld be dismissed. This time, the president gave in. Hours later, Bush announced that he had accepted Rumsfeld's resignation.

The ouster of Rumsfeld marked an early victory in Pelosi's strategy to end the war. As she would soon learn, it would be one of her few victories.

OPPOSING THE FIRST IRAQ WAR

In the summer of 1990, Pelosi had been in Congress less than four years when Iraqi dictator Saddam Hussein ordered his troops to cross Iraq's southern border into neighboring Kuwait. At the time, Iraq had just completed a long and devastating war against Iran with neither country making gains. The war had depleted Iraq's national treasury, but other Arab leaders rebuffed Saddam's calls for aid. And so Saddam turned his attention toward tiny, oil-rich Kuwait. For years, Saddam had bickered with the Kuwaitis, accusing them of dumping abundant quantities of oil onto the world petroleum market, thus keeping prices low. Saddam also suspected that the Kuwaitis were siphoning oil from Iraq's deposits—drilling diagonal wells from the Kuwait side of the border into Iraq territory. On August 2, 1990, Saddam sent his troops across the border, occupying Kuwaiti cities and taking over the country's oil fields.

The response by the United States and other Western nations was swift. President George H.W. Bush organized a coalition of nations, sending nearly 1 million troops to the Persian Gulf. For months, Bush demanded that the Iraqis leave Kuwait, but Saddam refused. On January 12, 1991, Congress voted to authorize the president to use force against the Iraqis. In the House, the resolution passed 250 to 183. Pelosi voted against the resolution. She believed that the administration had not pursued all diplomatic channels before resorting to the use of force.

Four days later, coalition aircraft swooped into Baghdad, bombing military installations and other strategic Iraqi positions. For more than a month, the planes pummeled the Iraqis, but Saddam refused to withdraw from Kuwait. On February 23, coalition ground forces entered Kuwait and quickly drove out the Iraqis. President Bush elected not to pursue the ground war into Iraq. By February 27, the fighting was over.

Coalition forces—about half of whom were American—had scored a decisive victory over the Iraqis. Twelve years later, as President Bush's son, George W. Bush, prepared a new invasion of Iraq, there was no reason to suspect that the war could not be won in a similarly decisive fashion.

PROPHETIC WORDS

Following the September 11, 2001, terrorist attacks, the Bush administration gathered evidence on Saddam, contending that the Iraqi dictator maintained close ties to al-Qaeda, the terrorist group that had engineered the Pentagon and World Trade Center attacks. Bush administration officials also disclosed that Saddam was gathering materials for a nuclear weapons program, specifically quantities of uranium mined in the African country of Niger. On February 6, 2003, Secretary of State Colin Powell made a convincing argument to the United Nations, contending that Saddam intended to build and use weapons of mass destruction.

Meanwhile, Bush had asked Congress for the authorization to invade Iraq. On October 10, 2002, the House voted 296 to 133 to authorize the use of force against Saddam. Again, Pelosi voted against war. Now the minority whip in the House, Pelosi said she was not convinced that Saddam maintained ties to al-Qaeda, nor did she believe the evidence suggesting that the Iraqi dictator maintained a nuclear weapons program. By then, American troops had invaded Afghanistan to topple the Taliban, the fundamentalist Islamic regime that harbored al-Qaeda leaders during the planning of the September 11 attacks. Pelosi said she was concerned that a massive invasion of Iraq would draw resources away from the fight in Afghanistan, which she believed was the true front in the war on terror. "The clear and present danger that threatens our country is terrorism," she said. "I say flat out that unilateral action against Iraq will be harmful to our war on terrorism."[2] Pelosi was the lone member of the Democratic leadership in the House to oppose the war; Minority Leader Richard Gephardt and other ranking Democrats supported the invasion.

Pelosi's words turned out to be prophetic—but not immediately. U.S. and British troops invaded Iraq on March 19, 2003. Within days, the Iraqi army was defeated and Saddam was on the run—he was later arrested, hiding in a ditch near the city of Tikrit. (Charged with crimes against his own people—systematic murders, rapes, tortures, and lootings—Saddam was tried in Iraq and then executed on December 30, 2006.) On May 1, 2003—just six weeks after the invasion—President Bush boarded the aircraft carrier *USS Abraham Lincoln* and, standing in front of a sign that said "Mission Accomplished," announced that major combat operations in Iraq had concluded.

By then, the American people were strongly in favor of the war. Indeed, Pelosi's opposition to the invasion seemed to be contrary to the overwhelming sentiment of Americans, but over time her staunch opposition to the war in Iraq would make her a key player in the strategy to withdraw American troops.

TROOP SURGE

Within months of the invasion, American inspectors concluded that Saddam had not maintained a nuclear weapons program. Nor did the Americans turn up evidence that he had supported al-Qaeda or the September 11 attacks. Meanwhile, conditions in Iraq deteriorated into a civil war, while the elected Iraqi government seemed powerless to stem the violence and govern effectively. Back home, Americans were divided. When the country stars the Dixie Chicks criticized Bush just before the invasion of Iraq, they were denounced by many of their fans. Later, they were regarded as heroes for being among the first celebrities to speak against the war. When filmmaker Michael Moore released his antiwar documentary *Fahrenheit 9/11*, critics accused him of liberal bias but were later astounded when the film earned nearly $120 million at the box office. Supporters of the war were further stunned in 2005 when Representative John Murtha of Pennsylvania, a Vietnam War veteran and major proponent of the Iraq invasion, suddenly announced his opposition and called for immediate troop withdrawals.

As public sentiment turned against the war and American casualties continually rose (by early 2008 more than 4,000

DID YOU KNOW?

Besides wielding the gavel as speaker of the House, Nancy Pelosi is also known to look for votes by baking chocolate cakes for House members. Indeed, as she climbed the ranks into the Democratic leadership, members who often provided her with key votes would find themselves rewarded with homemade chocolate cakes. Since becoming speaker, she has far less time to bake. Now, she often gives chocolate bars to supporters. In 2006, the *International Herald Tribune* labeled her a "chocolate-and-gavel leader."*

Some other facts about Pelosi:

- Her secret ambition is to be a singer, and her favorite singer is Barbra Streisand. She concedes, however, that she has no singing voice.
- Her husband, Paul, buys her clothes. Pelosi says she does not have time to do her own shopping and, besides, she does not like to shop.
- She enjoys solving crossword puzzles. She says, "I do crossword puzzles every day. I just love it. On Sundays,

American troops had died in Iraq), Bush refused to withdraw troops, although he did make one important concession to his critics: he appointed the Iraq Study Group, a blue-ribbon panel of foreign-policy experts whom he charged with developing a future strategy for Iraq.

Before the Iraq Study Group could issue its report, American voters responded to the situation in Iraq by ousting the GOP majority in Congress in the fall 2006 elections. On the day after the election, Bush acknowledged the loss, calling it a "thumpin'."[3] He quickly invited the new congressional leadership, Pelosi as well as Senate Majority

when I'm doing the *New York Times* crossword, nobody interrupts me. I'm in my own zone. That's my relaxation."**

- Her father, Mayor Tommy D'Alesandro, would not let her go out on a date unless he talked with her boyfriend first. On many occasions, she says, the mayor would give her date quite a grilling.
- Besides giving chocolates as gifts to supporters, Pelosi admits to harboring a chocolate addiction herself. In her office, visitors can find bowls of dark chocolate manufactured by Ghirardelli, a San Francisco-based chocolate company.

---

*Kate Zernike. "A Chocolate-and-Gavel Leader." *International Herald Tribune*, November 9, 2006. Available online at http://www.iht.com/articles/2006/11/09/news/pelosi.php.
**Thomas Fields-Meyer. "Lady of the House." *People*. Vol. 66 (Dec. 18, 2006): p. 81.

Leader Harry Reid of Nevada and other key Democrats, to the White House for a meeting. There, Pelosi and Reid made it clear to the president that they would oppose him on continuation of the war. House Majority Leader Steny Hoyer, who also attended the meeting, said, "[Pelosi] clearly made the point that the American people believe that what we are doing in Iraq is not working, and we need to address it. . . . The president said, 'I hope we can discuss that.' "[4]

Soon after the White House meeting, the Iraq Study Group issued its report and recommended strongly that the administration begin a gradual drawdown of troops. Bush rejected the notion and instead supported the concept of a surge—an increase of some 20,000 troops and a change in strategy aimed at quelling the violence on Iraqi streets. In Washington, the debate raged on the floor of the House, as Pelosi organized a coalition of war opponents who insisted that Congress establish a timetable for troop withdrawal.

Debate on the House floor stirred for weeks. One after another, Democrats and Republicans rose to give their positions for and against the troop surge. Most Democrats wanted to begin troop withdrawals, while most Republicans said they would continue to support the president. War proponents argued that drawing out troops before Iraq had been stabilized would lead to further violence and lawlessness, making Iraq a haven for terrorists. Democrats insisted, though, that Iraq had fallen into violence specifically because of the American presence there. What's more, they argued that Americans should not be placed in harm's way to support a regime that was simply not in control of the government. For her part, Pelosi charged that the Bush administration had failed to take a regional approach to ending the conflict by refusing to invite Iran, Syria, and other neighboring states into peace talks. She said, "In order to succeed in Iraq, there must be diplomatic and political initiatives. There has been no sustained and effective effort to engage Iraq's neighbors diplomatically, and there has been no sustained and effective effort to engage Iraqi factions politically. . . . President Bush's escalation proposal will not make Americans safer, will not make our military stronger, and will not make the region more stable. And it will not have my support."[5]

SETTING BENCHMARKS

To bring the debate to a head, Pelosi and other antiwar Democrats proposed a series of measures designed to force the issue on Iraq. The first measure was intended as a nonbinding resolution, simply giving the president the message that the House opposed Bush's plan for the surge. The vote occurred on February 16, 2007; the nonbinding resolution carried by a vote of 246 to 182. All but two Democrats backed the resolution. Seventeen Republicans broke ranks with their party to oppose the war. The president was unmoved.

Now, Pelosi and the Democrats prepared for a much more significant measure. Many members of the caucus demanded an immediate withdrawal of troops. Wary that the measure would not pass, Pelosi suggested instead that Congress set a deadline for withdrawal, linking the timetable to the funding Bush said he needed to continue the war. (Under law, the House approves all federal spending.) Pelosi and other House leaders crafted a bill authorizing $124 billion to continue financing the war, but with the caveat that the military would have to cease major combat operations by September 2007. The bill also required the Iraqi government to meet several benchmarks for establishing better civil control over the country.

On April 25, 2007, the bill came to the floor of the House for a vote. It passed by the razor-thin majority of 218 to 210. A day later, the Senate narrowly approved its version of the bill as well, but on May 1 the president vetoed the legislation.

Nancy Pelosi smiled to the applause of tour groups inside the Capitol on February 16, 2007, after the House voted in a nonbinding resolution to oppose President Bush's plans for a troop surge in Iraq. A later vote linking funding for the war with a timetable for troop withdrawal narrowly passed the House, but there were not enough votes to override the president's veto.

He insisted that the surge had been successful and called on Congress to pass a new war-spending plan with no strings attached. A day later, Pelosi scheduled a vote to override the veto, but the override measure fell 62 votes short of the two-thirds majority needed to adopt the legislation without the president's signature. Reluctantly, Pelosi met with Senate Majority Leader Harry Reid to craft a war-spending bill that included no deadline for withdrawal of troops.

IN HER OWN WORDS

When Nancy Pelosi spoke before the House on May 2, 2007, she called for an override of President Bush's veto of a bill that placed a timetable on American troop withdrawal from Iraq. The vote to override fell short of the two-thirds majority needed to adopt the legislation without the president's signature. Still, Pelosi suggested that opposition to the war would not end on that day. She said:

> The Congress will not support an open-ended commitment to a war without end. The President says he wants a blank check. The Congress will not give it to him.
>
> Next, the president said that Congress is substituting our judgment for the judgments of the commanders in the field 6,000 miles away. Wrong again, Mr. President. We're substituting our judgment for your judgment 16 blocks down Pennsylvania Avenue in the White House. We are substituting the judgment of this Congress for your failed judgment. The American people have lost faith in the president's conduct of the war. They have said that they want accountability and a new direction. This bill gives them both. . . .
>
> The president claims that this legislation "infringes upon the powers vested in the presidency by the Constitution." The president is wrong. Congress is exercising its right as a co-equal branch of government to work cooperatively with the president to end this war.
>
> By voting yes to override, Congress sends a strong message supporting our troops. They have done everything that has been asked of them and excellently. They deserve better. To rebuild our military, which has been seriously strained by this war in Iraq, to honor our commitment to our veterans, our heroes, and to demand accountability . . .
>
> Let us stop this war without end.

However, Pelosi and Reid did extract one major compromise from the White House—while not setting a timetable, the bill did set strict benchmarks for the Iraqi government to meet in establishing more control over the country's warring ethnic and religious factions. In a meeting on May 23 with other war opponents, Pelosi said, "I don't like this bill today. And when people call it a compromise, it's not really a compromise. We allowed it to come to the floor, but it's not as if we split the difference on the policy. The president, though, is having to accept accountability at least on the benchmarks that are there, so that's a step forward, and I do believe this represents a new direction. It's a small step."[6]

On May 24, the House passed the war-funding bill by a vote of 280 to 142. Pelosi refused to vote for the bill.

"BEGINNING OF THE END"

As the war entered its sixth year in 2008, supporters of the president insisted that the troop surge had been effective in reducing the amount of violence in Iraq. Critics of the war continued to harbor doubts, arguing that the Iraqi government failed to meet the benchmarks set by the legislation passed the previous May. Violence continued on Iraqi streets; each day, new casualties were reported among Iraqi civilians and American troops.

What's more, during the 2003 invasion the British had been charged with maintaining order in the southern Iraq city of Basra. At the outset, some 40,000 British troops had been deployed to Basra and nearby areas. By late 2007, most of Great Britain's troops had been withdrawn, but soon after the British withdrawal violence escalated in Basra. Elsewhere in the country, violence continued to flare as Sunni and Shiite militias vied for power.

Following the failure of the House to pass a bill setting a timeline for troop withdrawal, many antiwar activists complained that Pelosi and other Democratic leaders had

Members of the antiwar group Codepink protested against funding for the war in Iraq in March 2007 outside Nancy Pelosi's office on Capitol Hill. Antiwar activists were critical of Pelosi and other Democratic leaders for not standing up to President Bush.

let them down—that they had failed to stand up to Bush. One of Pelosi's harshest critics was Cindy Sheehan, the California woman who became a leader of the antiwar movement after her son died in Iraq. Until the House vote, Sheehan directed much of her activism against the president—in 2005, she maintained a 26-day vigil just outside the president's ranch in Crawford, Texas. Eventually, hundreds of protesters joined her in the vigil.

After the House vote, Sheehan aimed her rancor toward Pelosi. In fact, Sheehan said she planned to run against the speaker for her seat in the 2008 elections. "I'm doing it to encourage other people to run against Congress members who aren't doing their jobs," Sheehan said. "She (Pelosi) let the people down who worked hard to put Democrats back in power, who we thought were our hope for change."[7] Sheehan's campaign was not regarded as a serious threat to Pelosi's chances of winning re-election to the House; nevertheless, her candidacy underscored the emotional fervor many people harbor about the war in Iraq.

While Sheehan and other opponents of the war hold Democrats responsible for not ending the war, Pelosi's supporters point out that, before her elevation to speaker, the House was willing to give the president a blank check for the war. Since taking over, the Democrats have altered the national agenda on Iraq. Now, all political leaders in Washington must be prepared to talk about ways to end American involvement in Iraq. Said Murtha, "Through hearings and through monetary accountability, we're going to force them to recognize that we need to get out of there. Now, it's not going to happen overnight. It's going to take time. (Pelosi) works at it diligently. Pushing back, pushing back against the president when he says something. . . . It's political pressure exerted by a majority. And if you don't have a majority, none of this would be happening. I think the most important part is accountability. I think that's the most important thing she's taken on. It's going to have a real impact in the long run."[8]

Clearly, the fate of the American troops in Iraq will be in the hands of the American president who takes office in January 2009. In the meantime, opponents of the war in Congress took some satisfaction in knowing that President Bush was sent the message that the American people would no longer give him a blank check to continue fighting a war that only a minority of Americans seem willing to support. Soon after the May 24 vote that set benchmarks, Illinois Representative Rahm Emanuel said, "I view this as the beginning of the end of the president's policy on Iraq."[9]

"Impeachment Is off the Table"

During 2007 and 2008, as Nancy Pelosi traveled the country as speaker, she constantly encountered Democratic activists and others who demanded that she initiate impeachment proceedings against President George W. Bush and Vice President Dick Cheney. "I go through airports, and people have buttons as if they knew I was coming,"[1] Pelosi said.

Indeed, a movement to impeach Bush and Cheney had grown since the invasion of Iraq indicated that Saddam Hussein did not maintain a nuclear weapons program, which Bush used as evidence to justify the use of force in Iraq. As Bush sought permission from Congress to invade the Middle East nation, his aides produced documentation suggesting that Saddam had tried to obtain raw uranium from mines in the African nation of Niger.

Those allegations eventually proved false. As such, several members of Congress believed Bush lied to them about Saddam's weapons program, which they maintain is an impeachable offense. They also believed that Bush's authorization of wiretaps on suspected terror suspects without the court-approved warrants ordinarily required for domestic spying was a violation of the law. Cheney had also been singled out as a candidate for impeachment. Critics suggested that he broke the law when he allegedly authorized aides to leak the name of Central Intelligence Agency official Valerie Plame Wilson to reporters. Wilson's husband, former diplomat Joseph Wilson, is an outspoken critic of the war, and critics suggested that Cheney ordered the disclosure of his wife's name as retribution for Wilson's criticism. Finally, as evidence surfaced suggesting that Bush, Cheney, and other top administration officials condoned the use of "waterboarding" and other questionable methods of interrogating terror suspects, calls for impeachment resumed. Waterboarding is an interrogation technique that makes the suspect believe he is drowning. Critics of the technique regard waterboarding as a form of torture.

"The president and vice president . . . used deception to drive us into the Iraq War, claiming Saddam Hussein and al-Qaeda were in cahoots, when they knew better," said Elizabeth Holtzman, a former member of Congress who voted in 1974 to recommend the impeachment of President Richard M. Nixon. "They invoked the specter of a nuclear attack on the United States, alleging Hussein purchased uranium from Niger and wanted aluminum tubes for uranium enrichment, when they had every reason to know these claims were phony or at least seriously questioned within the administration. Withholding and distorting facts usurps Congress's constitutional power to decide on going to war."[2]

As the speaker of the U.S. House, Pelosi would be in a position to authorize the commencement of impeachment proceedings. Under law, all impeachment cases begin in the House.

AMERICANS FAVOR IMPEACHMENT

As outlined in the U.S. Constitution, impeachment provides Congress with a process to remove from office a federal official who has committed "treason, bribery, or other high crimes and misdemeanors."[3] It has been invoked only a handful of times in U.S. history, most notably in cases of impeachment brought against Presidents Andrew Johnson in 1868 and Bill Clinton in 1998. In both cases, after trial in the Senate, neither president was found to have committed impeachable offenses and both remained in office. In 1974, the House Judiciary Committee voted to recommend articles of impeachment against Nixon, but the president resigned before the full House voted on the measure.

The first step in impeachment is an investigation by the House Judiciary Committee, usually conducted through a series of hearings. If the committee develops evidence of an impeachable offense, the panel drafts articles of impeachment against the officeholder. If approved by the entire House, the procedure moves to the Senate for a trial. At the conclusion of the trial, the Senate votes on the guilt or innocence of the officeholder. Conviction requires a two-thirds majority vote of the Senate.

During the first six years of the Bush administration, when the Republican Party held power in the House, impeachment was never seriously considered, but when the Democrats took control of the chamber following the 2006 elections, the calls for impeachment suddenly gained fervor. Indeed, a poll commissioned in late 2005 by the activist organization AfterDowningStreet.org suggested that 53 percent of Americans favored impeachment of Bush if the president was found to have lied about the reasons for going to war in Iraq. Said John Nichols, Washington correspondent for the political journal *The Nation*, "The election of a president does not make him a king for four years. . . . If a president sins against the Constitution—and does damage to the republic—the people have a right in an organic process to demand of their House of Representatives, the branch of government closest to the people, that it act to remove that president. And I think that sentiment is afoot in the land."[4]

AfterDowningStreet.org took its name from the so-called Downing Street Memo, a document issued by the British prime minister's office at 10 Downing Street in London that was leaked to British newspapers. The memorandum suggested that Bush planned to invade Iraq as early as 2002. After the group released the results of its poll, AfterDowningStreet.org co-founder Bob Fertik said, "These results are stunning. A clear majority of Americans now supports President Bush's impeachment if he lied about the war. This should send shock waves through the White House—and a wake-up call to Democrats and Republicans in Congress, who have the sole power under the Constitution to impeach President Bush."[5]

SERIOUS QUESTIONS

Members of Congress took notice. Even before the 2006 elections, some influential Democrats in Congress started to circulate proposed resolutions to begin investigations of the president's conduct in the months leading up to the 2003 invasion of Iraq. Meanwhile, in the Senate, Wisconsin Democrat Russell Feingold offered a resolution to "censure" Bush for approving the warrantless wiretaps. A censure is a far less severe form of punishment than impeachment. Under a censure, the officeholder is issued a public reprimand. By censuring the president, the Senate would merely

In 2006, before Democrats had won back the House, Representative John Conyers *(center)* had put forth a resolution to investigate the president's conduct leading up to the war in Iraq. Nancy Pelosi, though, was worried that impeachment could become a divisive battle.

issue a formal condemnation of Bush's conduct and seek no further punishment. Feingold found little support for his resolution to censure, as only Democrats Barbara Boxer of California and Tom Harkin of Iowa signed the resolution.

In the House, though, a much more aggressive campaign was under way. Michigan Democrat John Conyers Jr.—the ranking Democrat on the Judiciary Committee—circulated a resolution that would initiate an investigation of the president. By early 2006, 29 other members of the House had signed on as cosponsors. One cosponsor had been Representative Zoe Lofgren of California, who said, "Serious questions have been raised about President Bush's actions in approving warrantless wiretaps by the NSA

(National Security Agency), as well as questions about both the vice president's and president's information that was provided to the Congress on the basis for the decision to initiate war in Iraq. These important questions need to be answered."[6]

The fact that Conyers was the original sponsor of the resolution calling for an investigation was significant. After the 2006 election, Conyers became chairman of the House Judiciary Committee. If the House moved toward impeachment, Conyers would have a major influence over the charges filed against the president and the vice president.

LEADERSHIP VACUUM

As Pelosi weighed the arguments for and against impeachment, she could not help but remember what occurred in the House during the 1998 impeachment of President Clinton. There is no question that the controversy over the Clinton impeachment divided the country. For years, Clinton had been under investigation by independent counsel Kenneth Starr for a questionable real estate venture known as Whitewater that occurred while Clinton was governor of Arkansas. By 1998, the investigation appeared to be stalled with no evidence of impropriety by the president. However, unrelated to the Whitewater case, a former state government worker in Arkansas, Paula Jones, had filed a lawsuit against Clinton, claiming he had sexually harassed her. While giving a deposition in the case—a pretrial interview conducted by attorneys—Clinton was asked by Jones's lawyers whether he had engaged in a romantic liaison with a young White House intern, Monica Lewinsky. Clinton denied that he had maintained a relationship with the woman. Unknown to Clinton, though, Lewinsky had been talking about the affair with a friend, Linda Tripp, who secretly taped her phone calls with the intern. Tripp turned the tapes over to Starr.

Based on the contradictory evidence provided by the Lewinsky tapes, Starr recommended that charges of obstruction of justice and perjury—lying under oath in a civil case—be brought against the president.

Republican leaders in the House seized on the opportunity to embarrass the president. The GOP-led House Judiciary Committee convened hearings and quickly authorized articles of impeachment against Clinton, maintaining that lying under oath was an impeachable offense. The full House voted on the articles in late 1998, authorizing the impeachment by a narrow margin. Outside Washington, talk of the case could be found in every corner of society as Americans faced the possibility that a twice-elected president could be ousted from office for the offense of lying about a secret liaison with a young woman. Although the president's popularity plummeted, many people rose to his defense, insisting that the issue of whether Clinton committed adultery should be a matter between the president and his wife, first lady Hillary Clinton, and not the subject of impeachment and trial.

What's more, the impeachment had a definite partisan flavor. The House vote authorizing the impeachment essentially broke along party lines. Following the House vote, a three-week trial was held in the Senate, where Republican House members presented the case against the president. Observers expected the Senate vote to break along party lines as well. Indeed, Republicans held a slight majority in the Senate but they did not hold enough of a majority to ensure the two-thirds of the chamber—67 votes—needed for conviction. At the conclusion of the trial, just 45 senators voted for conviction on the perjury charge while 50 voted for conviction on the obstruction-of-justice charge. Clinton was acquitted and permitted to remain in office for the conclusion of his presidency.

(continues on page 94)

THE HISTORY OF IMPEACHMENT

In the United States, the concept of impeachment was first raised in the Federalist Papers, the essays authored by Alexander Hamilton, James Madison, and John Jay in the months leading up to ratification of the U.S. Constitution. In Federalist No. 65, Hamilton suggested that the new Constitution include a process of impeachment in a "method of national inquest into the conduct of public men."* Clearly, the framers of the Constitution wished to establish a method to remove officials who engaged in criminal conduct. The role of the House in impeachment as well as the Senate's responsibility to hold a trial are outlined in Article I of the Constitution.

The first official to be impeached was John Pickering, a federal judge from New Hampshire. He was impeached and kicked out of office in 1804 for habitual drunkenness. Since then, 12 judges—including Supreme Court Associate Justice Samuel Chase—one Cabinet officer and two presidents have been impeached. Chase was charged with being unfair to trial participants but acquitted. The Cabinet officer, Secretary of War William Belknap, was impeached for taking bribes. He was acquitted in the Senate but resigned. The presidents, Andrew Johnson and Bill Clinton, were both acquitted at their trials. Johnson was impeached when his enemies claimed he violated federal law by trying to fire Secretary of War William Stanton. He was acquitted by a single vote in the Senate. Clinton was impeached for lying under oath about an intimate relationship with a White House intern, but the Senate vote after his trial fell short of conviction.

In 1974, the House Judiciary Committee voted to recommend articles of impeachment against President

Richard M. Nixon, but Nixon resigned before the full House voted. The case against Nixon grew out of the Watergate scandal, in which operatives in the employ of Nixon's re-election committee were caught planting electronic eavesdropping devices in the headquarters of the Democratic National Committee in the Watergate hotel in Washington. In the months following the June 1972 break-in, a series of investigative articles in newspapers as well as a probe by a special prosecutor uncovered a program of spying and dirty tricks by the re-election committee. When Nixon's voice was recorded on his Oval Office taping system discussing a cover-up of the Watergate break-in, the House Judiciary Committee believed it had found the evidence it needed to impeach the president.

Said Elizabeth Holtzman, a former member of Congress from New York who served on the Judiciary Committee during the Watergate hearings, "The Constitution specifies the grounds as treason, bribery or 'high crimes and misdemeanors,' a term that means 'great and dangerous offenses that subvert the Constitution.' As the House Judiciary Committee determined during Watergate, impeachment is warranted when a president puts himself above the law and gravely abuses power."**

**Bill Moyers Journal*. PBS, July 13, 2007. Available online at http://www.pbs.org/moyers/journal/07132007/impeachment.html.

** Elizabeth Holtzman. "Judiciary Committee Should Move to Impeach Bush and Cheney." *The Philadelphia Inquirer*, January 27, 2008, p. D-6.

(continued from page 91)

And so the president survived the impeachment, but the same could not be said for Republican leaders of the House. The speaker of the House who permitted the impeachment vote on Clinton to come to the floor was Republican Newt Gingrich of Georgia. During the controversy, Gingrich's popularity plummeted. The public also lost confidence in the Republican majority in the House, viewing the impeachment as a mean-spirited GOP maneuver. In the November 1998 elections, voters punished the Republicans by reducing their majority in the chamber by five seats. Following the 1998 election, Gingrich resigned from the House. He was to have been succeeded as speaker by Bob Livingston, a Republican from Louisiana, but before Livingston had the opportunity to be officially voted in by the Republican caucus, a national magazine reported that Livingston had also had extramarital affairs. After the revelations, which further eroded the public's confidence in the Republican House leadership, Livingston was forced to resign as well.

Nearly a decade later, as talk about the possible impeachments of Bush and Cheney swirled around Washington, no one needed to remind Nancy Pelosi that impeachment could develop into a divisive and partisan battle, splitting the country, eroding the public's confidence in Congress, and throwing the House into a leadership vacuum.

CHECKS AND BALANCES

Across the country, several city councils and other municipal governments passed resolutions asking Congress to consider impeachment. Indeed, one governing body that asked the Congress to initiate an investigation of the president and vice president was the Board of Supervisors in San Francisco, a council that expected its message to resonate with the speaker.

As the 2006 elections approached, Pelosi spoke carefully whenever she was asked about impeachment of Bush and Cheney. She was well aware that an impeachment case could backfire, and she did not want to jeopardize her party's chances to recapture the majority at the polls that fall. Appearing on the NBC news show *Meet the Press* in May 2006, host Tim Russert asked her about the Conyers resolution. "Is impeachment off the table?"[7] Russert asked.

"Well, you never know where the facts take you," Pelosi answered, "but . . . that isn't what we're about. What we're about is going there and having high ethical standards, fiscal soundness, and a level of civility that brushes away all this fierce partisanship."[8] Clearly, Pelosi was concerned that Democrats would face a backlash if they pursued an impeachment case that proved to be unpopular. Mindful of the support that Americans had given to President Clinton during his impeachment battles with the Republican Congress, Pelosi decided to suppress impeachment efforts in the House. "Impeachment is off the table,"[9] she asserted.

Proponents of impeachment reacted bitterly. AfterDowningStreet.org spokesman David Swanson charged that Pelosi had put the fortunes of the Democratic Party ahead of the Congress's constitutionally mandated job of pursuing articles of impeachment against a president and a vice president who may have broken the law. Swanson said, "She's thinking in terms of the election. It's disgraceful to put electoral politics ahead of checks and balances and the Constitution."[10]

"People don't want to let this go," added John Nichols, the journalist for *The Nation*. "They do not accept Nancy Pelosi's argument that impeachment is 'off the table.' Because I guess maybe they're glad she didn't take some other part of the Constitution off the table like freedom of speech. But they also don't hold the argument that, oh

A protester wearing a George Bush mask demonstrated in February 2008 outside a hotel in Plainsboro, New Jersey, where Nancy Pelosi was appearing. The protesters were upset that Pelosi had not moved to bring impeachment hearings against the president and the vice president.

well . . . let's just hold our breath till Bush and Cheney get done."[11]

Others believed that Pelosi was simply being practical. They pointed out that, even if the House Judiciary Committee uncovered impeachable evidence against Bush and Cheney, the Democrats enjoyed just the thinnest of majorities in the Senate. Like the Republicans in the 1999 impeachment trial of Clinton, the Democrats would never be able to muster a two-thirds majority to convict the president and the vice president. What's more, as the impeachment argument dragged into 2008, critics pointed out that there simply would not be enough time to launch an investigation and hold hearings in the House and a trial in the Senate before Bush and Cheney left office in early 2009. Said Michael Tomasky, an American editor for the British newspaper *The Guardian*, "I understand Democrats' impatience with their party's leaders in Congress. Demand that they de-fund the war if you wish . . . but if you're asking them to impeach, you're asking them to undertake an effort that's bound to fail and for which there's no time anyway."[12]

QUESTIONS REMAIN

Nevertheless, questions about impeachment continued to surface in 2008. In the small town of Brattleboro, Vermont, activists staged a referendum calling for the immediate arrest and prosecution of Bush and Cheney should either of them set foot in the community. The referendum was nonbinding and regarded as strictly ceremonial—if adopted, it could not be enforced. Nevertheless, on March 4, nearly 4,000 Brattleboro residents went to the polls and adopted the referendum. Said Kurt Daims, the Brattleboro man who persuaded the town council to slate the ballot question, "I hope the one thing that people take from this is, 'Hey, it can be done.'"[13] Impeachment campaigns surfaced in other communities. In New Hampshire, a state lawmaker introduced a resolution calling for the legislature to endorse the impeachments of the president and the vice president.

Through it all, though, Pelosi stood steadfast against efforts to initiate an impeachment investigation, maintaining that a trial of the president and vice president would divide the country. "It was my belief that an impeachment of the vice president or the president . . . would be very divisive in our country, and that is what I believed (in 2006)," Pelosi said. "It should have come (as) no surprise when I became speaker (that) I said it again, and I continue to hold that view."[14]

Breaking Through the Gridlock

By the end of her first year as speaker, Nancy Pelosi had a record that included some clear victories but also some defeats. She had engineered a raise in the minimum wage, instituted a number of ethics reforms for members of Congress, and instituted energy-saving measures in the House itself—that holiday season, the Capitol Christmas tree was decorated with energy-efficient light-emitting diode bulbs rather than conventional incandescent bulbs, which sap more electricity.

There were many defeats, though, including her attempt to recognize the Armenian genocide and her efforts to fund embryonic stem cell research. But it was Pelosi's failure to rein in the president on the war in Iraq that frustrated her the most and helped turn public hostility away from the president and toward Congress. At the end of 2007, Pelosi said, "The war in Iraq is the biggest disappointment for us."[1]

After Democratic lawmakers caved in to the president on the war, polls showed that the public approval rating for Congress dropped to 18 percent—the lowest rating for Congress in 15 years. By the summer of 2007, *USA Today* reported, "That 'honeymoon' period for the new Democratically controlled Congress was brief, as its job ratings dropped below 30 percent in March 2007 and have now fallen below where they were just before the Democrats took over."[2]

Bush was able to stall the Democratic agenda because he managed to keep the allegiance of most Republicans in Congress. Indeed, the 2006 elections provided Democrats with just slim majorities in the House and the Senate—particularly in the Senate, where Democrats enjoyed just a one-vote margin. Democratic defections on major bills were common while, on the GOP side, Republican senators rarely broke ranks. "What is interesting to me is how the Republicans have stuck with the president," Pelosi said in December 2007. "I didn't foresee that."[3]

THE CHILDREN'S HEALTH BILL

No place was Republican allegiance to the president more evident than on a bill to expand free health-care coverage to more children. Under legislation proposed by the Democrats, Congress would add $35 billion to the State Children's Health Insurance Program over five years, bringing the total funding for the program to $60 billion. The program already serves about 6 million children a year from low-income families. By expanding the program, Democrats hoped to deliver free health care to an additional 4 million children a year. "To be a great nation," Pelosi said, "we have to take care of the health of our children. It should almost go without saying, but it doesn't. There is every compassionate, humanitarian, motherly, fatherly, and family reason to be for this legislation. It also makes good economic sense."[4]

Bush opposed the legislation, insisting that it expanded free health care to families that should be able to afford medical expenses without government assistance. He vowed to veto the bill if it passed Congress. On Sept. 26, 2007, the House passed the legislation by a vote of 265 to 159—26 votes shy of the two-thirds majority proponents would need to override the president's veto.

The Senate passed the bill and, as expected, the president vetoed the legislation. Pelosi and other Democratic leaders in the House mapped out a strategy to override the president's veto. They encouraged supporters of the legislation to hold rallies. Public interest groups financed radio and television commercials, calling on people to contact their members of Congress and urge them to override the veto. The public campaign seemed to be working—polls showed most Americans favored an expansion of the children's health program.

Meanwhile, on Capitol Hill, the Democrats targeted several Republicans from so-called swing districts who they believed would be willing to cross party lines on the legislation. (A swing district is a congressional district where Republicans and Democrats are registered in roughly equal numbers. Therefore, representatives from those districts are more likely to cross party lines since their constituents are likely to vote either way.) Pelosi and the others made dozens of phone calls to the swing-district Republicans, hoping to persuade them to change their minds.

The vote to override the president's veto was held on October 17. Despite ramping up the pressure on the

A disappointed Nancy Pelosi appeared at a news conference in October 2007 after the House failed to override a veto by President Bush to increase spending for the State Children's Health Insurance Program. With Pelosi is Representative Rahm Emanuel of Illinois.

swing-district Republicans, the vote to override fell short. Pelosi fumed over the refusal of Bush and the Republicans to budge. "This legislation will haunt (Bush) again and again and again," she declared. "It's not going away, because the children are not going away."[5]

Over in the Senate, Democratic leaders were finding themselves just as frustrated. In the Senate, Democrats lacked the 60 votes they needed to break filibusters, a tactic that senators can use to delay bills from coming to the floor. As a result, Republican leaders in the Senate were able to bottle up Democratic initiatives. Representative Howard L. Berman, a Democrat from California, said, "We have custody of Congress, but we don't have control. Bush has shown, time and again, that he's a very stubborn guy."[6]

With the Republicans refusing to budge on key policy issues and the Democrats unable to push through their

WHAT IS A VETO?

Under the U.S. Constitution, the president has 10 days to sign into law a bill that has been approved by both houses of Congress. If the president disagrees with the bill, the president has the option of returning the bill to the house where it originated, usually with a written explanation of why he or she won't sign it.

The Constitution provides a mechanism for Congress to enact a law without the president's signature: Each chamber must vote by a two-thirds majority to override the veto. If Congress fails to override the veto, leaders of the House and Senate may confer with the president to hammer out a compromise and then bring the new bill back to their chambers for new votes.

If Congress adjourns within the president's 10-day window, the president can still veto the bill without sending the bill back to Congress. In such cases, the president simply does nothing. This is known as a pocket veto. Congress does not have the power to override a pocket veto.

By early 2008, President George W. Bush had vetoed just nine bills. Only once was Congress able to override the president's veto—on a measure to provide $23 billion to fix municipal water-supply systems. On other issues, such as the use of federal funds for embryonic stem cell research and setting agenda, Congress settled into a period of stagnation known on Capitol Hill as gridlock. In cities, gridlock occurs when cars and trucks get stuck in traffic congestion, clogging busy intersections. Nothing can move, and life in the city

timelines for troop withdrawals from Iraq—Congress fell short of the two-thirds majority to override Bush's vetoes.

In contrast, other presidents have used their veto power much more aggressively. Franklin D. Roosevelt vetoed 635 bills sent to him by Congress. Grover Cleveland vetoed 414 bills. Gerald R. Ford, who served just a little more than two years in the White House, vetoed 68 bills.

Many presidential scholars believe the veto is a tactic that presidents would do well to use sparingly. They argue that presidents who veto a lot of legislation tend to make a lot of enemies in Congress. Says Robert Spitzer, a political science professor at the State University of New York at Cortland, "If you rely too much on the veto and not enough on constructive bargaining with Congress, it eggs Congress on to be more confrontational. After a while, the country begins to view the president in purely negative terms."*

Successful votes to override vetoes are rare in Congress. Out of nearly 1,500 presidential vetoes dating back to George Washington, Congress has overridden just a little more than 100.

---

*James N. Thurman. "Perils of Wielding a Veto Pen." *Christian Science Monitor*. Vol. 90 (June 25, 1998): p. 3.

seems to slow to a standstill. Meanwhile, frustration builds and tempers flare. And that pretty well sums up gridlock on Capitol Hill, too.

PROTECTING THE AUTOMAKERS

As Democrats and Republicans spent the year sparring on Capitol Hill, the availability of energy, particularly oil, became a major issue. For starters, scientists had been warning for years that the Earth was facing climate change, largely because of carbon emissions generated by automobiles. In Washington, Bush spent much of his administration ignoring the warnings, even as the public started to demand action that would curb global warming. According to environmentalists, the carbon produced by burning oil and other fossil fuels, such as coal and natural gas, acts as a "greenhouse gas," trapping the sun's radiation in the atmosphere. That has led to global warming, which over time can have a disastrous effect on the environment, including the melting of polar ice and a change in the ecosystems that support plant and animal life.

Meanwhile, the availability of energy became a concern as well. Not only were fossil fuels fouling the environment, but the world's demand for energy had created an international shortage. That fact became apparent to Americans as gasoline rose above $3 per gallon. Clearly, the United States needed a new energy policy.

Pelosi and the other leaders on Capitol Hill started to talk about an energy bill early in 2007. Pelosi favored tough fuel-efficiency standards for automobiles and other vehicles. Under the proposed legislation, automakers would have to improve the fuel efficiency in cars—making them go longer distances per gallon of gasoline. To Pelosi's consternation, she found initial opposition to the bill coming not from the White House or the Republican leadership in Congress, but from within the House

Democratic leadership. Democrat John D. Dingell, who represents a congressional district in Michigan, opposed the higher efficiency standards for automobiles. First elected to Congress in 1955, Dingell has scrupulously looked out for the interests of the nation's automobile manufacturers, who are largely based in Detroit and nearby communities. In Michigan, hundreds of thousands of people rely on the automakers for their livelihoods. Under the proposed legislation, automakers would have to spend tens of millions of dollars on research and development of more fuel-efficient engines—a circumstance that Dingell feared would force them to lay off thousands of manufacturing workers in order to pay for the new technology.

Energy-related legislation is generated by the House Energy and Commerce Committee, which regulates both the energy and automotive industries. Following the Democratic takeover of Congress in 2007, Dingell was named chairman of the panel. Clearly, any legislation that would affect the automobile industry would have to earn Dingell's approval.

In fact, the first legislation written by Dingell's committee was a much watered-down version of the sweeping energy bill that Pelosi hoped Congress would produce. Dingell wiped out a requirement for higher fuel-efficiency standards for the so-called sport utility vehicles, or SUVs, which had come to dominate the automotive market in the United States. At the time, newly manufactured SUVs and pickup trucks needed to achieve efficiency standards of only 21.6 miles per gallon of gasoline, while most other cars had to average 27.5 miles per gallon. Pelosi had hoped Dingell's committee would boost that standard to 35 miles per gallon on all types of vehicles.

Dingell refused to compromise. Throughout the summer and into the fall, the Energy and Commerce Committee worked on the bill. Pelosi tried a number of legislative maneuvers, mostly by placing pressure on other members of the Energy and Commerce Committee to hike efficiency standards, but the lawmakers were unwilling to cross the powerful chairman. "I've had conflicts with speakers before," Dingell told reporters. "This is not the first time."[7]

As the standoff between Dingell and Pelosi continued, prices at the gasoline pumps continued to rise. On the international oil market, the price of crude oil rose to nearly $100 a barrel—doubling in price in just four years. Meanwhile, the media continually reported new articles and concerns about the effects of global warming. Across America, city and state governments passed resolutions calling for the United States to adopt a new energy policy. In October 2007, as members of Congress prepared to debate the energy bill, former Vice President Al Gore as well as the United Nations Intergovernmental Panel on Climate Change were awarded the Nobel Peace Prize for their efforts to raise awareness of the dangers of climate change. A few months earlier, Gore's global-warming documentary *An Inconvenient Truth* won an Academy Award. Addressing a joint House-Senate committee investigating climate change, Gore said, "A day will come when our children and grandchildren will look back and they'll ask one of two questions. Either they will ask, 'What in God's name were they doing?' or they will say, 'How did they find the uncommon moral courage to rise above politics and redeem the promise of American democracy?' "[8] Clearly, many Americans wanted Congress to break the gridlock and pass a meaningful energy bill.

CONCERNS ABOUT ETHANOL

Finally, in November, Dingell offered a compromise. The chairman said he would be willing to support a fuel-efficiency standard of 35 miles per gallon for all new vehicles. SUVs and light trucks could dip below the standard, as long as the fleet of all cars sold in the United States burned fuel at the 35-mile-per-gallon standard. In other words, Dingell suggested that higher standards for smaller cars could offset a lower standard for the larger vehicles.

Dingell's approval of the legislation was just the first step toward resolving problems with the energy bill. Other Democrats opposed components of the bill, particularly those that addressed the use of ethanol in the production of gasoline.

Ethanol, which is regarded as an alternative fuel, is an alcohol-based substance that can be distilled from switch grass, sugarcane, corn, and other farm crops. Starting in 1978, Congress has provided tax breaks to oil companies that use ethanol as an additive to gasoline. Proponents of ethanol argue that it is cleaner burning and cheaper than petroleum and that its use helps reduce America's dependence on oil produced in the volatile Middle East.

However, ethanol does not have the overwhelming support of environmentalists and others. They argue that using farmland to produce ethanol-yielding crops means there is less farmland available to produce food. What's more, when farmers grow crops for food they must adhere to strict laws regarding the use of pesticides and fertilizers. Many of those rules do not apply when the crops are grown for purposes other than food, prompting environmentalists to worry that pesticides and fertilizers used to treat ethanol-producing crops would foul the soil.

Also, by diverting corn and other crops to fuel, prices for those crops will rise, causing prices for food to rise in the supermarkets. Members of Congress representing lower-income people in big cities wanted some protection against rising food prices. Meanwhile, Democrats who represented farm states demanded that more incentives be written into the legislation to benefit farmers who grow ethanol-yielding crops. (And even farm-state lawmakers were not united on the legislation—members of Congress who represented states where the cattle industry is significant oppose the use of ethanol because it drives up the price for feed corn.) Observers looked at the brewing stalemate and wondered how Pelosi would resolve the differences. "How she marries these various interests is really a challenge," said Melinda Price, a lobbyist for the Sierra Club, an environmental group. "The Democratic Party pie gets sliced differently every time, but it's the leader's job to figure out how to put it all together."[9]

Ultimately, Pelosi sided with the ethanol producers. She insisted that ethanol and other biofuels must be used to reduce carbon emissions and decrease American dependence on Middle East oil. "(We) have an approach that says that America's farmers will fuel America's energy independence," she said. "We will send our energy dollars not to the Middle East but to . . . the Midwest and to rural America."[10] When the legislation was completed, the authors included language mandating a fivefold increase of ethanol and other alternative fuels in gasoline by 2022.

RELUCTANT COMPROMISE

On December 6, 2007, the House passed the energy bill, a 1,055-page document that substantially changed the way energy is produced and used in the United States. Besides raising fuel-efficiency standards for American cars and making more use of biofuels, the legislation reduced greenhouse gas emissions from factory smokestacks and mandated the production of energy-saving light bulbs. Even commuters who ride their bicycles to work were addressed in the legislation—the new law gave them a tax break for not using their cars. The bill also made money available to cities to build projects that do not emit greenhouse gases. Finally, under the terms of the legislation, oil companies lost some

Nancy Pelosi's signature is affixed to H.R. 6-310, the energy bill that raised fuel-efficiency standards for U.S. automobiles and boosted the use of biofuels. Over the course of several months, Pelosi had to work out compromises with the president as well as members of her own party to come up with legislation that would pass.

$13 billion a year in tax breaks. (For years, Congress had granted oil companies tax relief for using some of their profits to explore for new sources of oil, but as the price of oil zoomed upward, so did the profits of the oil companies. As some of the major oil companies reported profits in the tens of billions of dollars, members of Congress had grown skeptical of the oil companies' intentions and vowed to repeal the tax breaks.)

The bill was largely written without input from Republicans in Congress, who fumed over being excluded from the process. "I can guarantee you that few, if any, of this body have read this bill,"[11] said Republican Jeff Flake of Arizona. At the White House, Bush threatened a veto, warning that he would not approve the bill unless the tax breaks to the oil companies were restored. In the Senate, Democratic leaders, fearing that they would again fall short of overriding a presidential veto, restored the tax breaks to the oil companies. Back in the House, Pelosi reluctantly agreed to the new bill. The revised version passed the House again, and on Dec. 18, the president signed the bill into law. "This . . . legislation will be a shot heard 'round the world for energy independence for America," Pelosi declared. "This is about our national security, it's about jobs and the economic security of our country, it's about the environment, therefore it's a health issue, and it's a moral issue."[12]

By shepherding the energy bill through Congress, Pelosi was able to break the Capitol Hill gridlock on a significant piece of legislation that is likely to improve the lives of generations of Americans. Still, it had taken Congress most of the year to craft the bill. Pelosi had to compromise with members of her own party as well as the president. As the year drew to a close, and the speaker and other congressional leaders were putting the finishing touches on the energy legislation, another crisis surfaced in the United States. This time, lawmakers would have little time to address the crisis, and they would also find themselves with little room to compromise.

Rescuing the Economy

For Nancy Pelosi, the energy bill represented a major accomplishment, showing that she could use her authority as House speaker to break the gridlock on Capitol Hill. What's more, adoption of the legislation proved that the speaker could react to a crisis and forge a compromise on important legislation. The energy bill, though, had taken months of negotiations before all the parties were satisfied with the compromise. In late 2007, when it became clear that the country was heading into an economic downturn, Pelosi and other leaders in Washington knew they would have to react to the new crisis, and they also knew that Americans could not wait long for a solution.

Across the United States, prices rose for food, gasoline, and other consumer goods. As businesses suffered, they started to lay off workers. On Wall Street, stock prices tumbled, meaning that most people's savings were worth less. In Washington, Pelosi wondered whether President George W. Bush had a plan to resuscitate the troubled economy and rescue the country from a recession. Said Pelosi, "Any homemaker in America could have told him months ago that our country was heading for a downturn, and we needed a change in economic policy."[1]

A recession occurs when the economy of the United States shrinks for two or more successive quarters, a span of time equal to at least six months. During a recession, most companies show little or no profits. It is far more likely that they will show losses—in other words, they lose money. To cut their losses, businesses trim their payrolls, meaning they lay off workers. When unemployment rises, a whole series of ills usually follow. With more people out of work, there is less spending on food, automobiles, consumer products and, particularly, homes. With less money spent in the American economy, companies have a harder time showing profits. Sometimes, it takes many months or even years for the economy to recover from a recession. The worst period of economic decline in American history started in 1929 and lasted into the early 1940s; it took a dozen years for the economy to recover from the long-term economic downturn, an era known to Americans as the Great Depression.

SUBPRIME MELTDOWN

There were a lot of factors causing the economic slowdown of 2007 and 2008, but chief among them was probably the failure of the subprime mortgage market. During the 1990s, a boom time in the American economy, housing prices escalated at a tremendous rate. To make homes affordable to Americans, many banks and mortgage companies offered mortgages in which the interest rates were below what is known as the "prime lending rate," which is the lowest interest rate available, usually reserved for the most credit-worthy borrowers only. Under the terms of the subprime mortgages, the initial interest rates—the money banks and mortgage companies charge customers for making loans—were kept artificially low. Also, the banks and mortgage companies did not demand large down payments from the borrowers. It meant young families with little money could buy expensive homes that they otherwise would not be able to afford.

For most new homeowners, that tenuous bit of financing seemed to work at first, but within two or three years the interest rates suddenly shot sky high as the banks and mortgage companies demanded paybacks for their subprime deals. Very quickly, people found themselves spending most of their money on mortgage payments. Eventually, many people were unable to make the monthly payments on their mortgages. They faced foreclosure, meaning the lenders seized their homes. With people unable to make mortgage payments and afford homes, the market for housing soon evaporated. By 2007, few people were able to buy homes, causing the prices for all housing to drop. New home construction slowed to a virtual standstill. Construction workers found themselves out of work. Suppliers of goods and services to the housing market—lumber companies, manufacturers of wire and other electrical components, plumbing suppliers, carpet companies, appliance makers, paint and wallpaper companies, landscaping suppliers and hundreds of other businesses related to housing—all saw their profits dry up as well.

Soon, the problems related to housing spilled over into other segments of the economy. Banks that shouldered huge losses when people defaulted on their mortgage payments were unable to make loans for other purposes. That meant most businesses seeking loans to expand were unable to find money available for those purposes. Meanwhile,

A foreclosure sign sits in front of a house in Spring Valley, California, in the fall of 2007. Across the country, many people were having problems meeting their mortgage payments, and prices for food and gas were on the rise as well. To quickly address the economic downturn, Congress would need to overcome partisan gridlock.

with many people unable to pay their mortgages, they were also hard-pressed to pay other loans as well—particularly the balances they were carrying on their credit cards. Many people were facing a downward spiral into unemployment and relentless debt.

In early January 2008, Treasury Secretary Henry Paulson took a gauge of several corporate executives, particularly those who run large retail companies, to see whether the Christmas shopping season had sparked the economy. The responses to Paulson's inquiries were rather pessimistic. "Everybody is telling me that things took a downturn in the middle of December,"[2] Paulson reported. By that point, most officials in Washington were forced to admit that the country was heading for a recession, if not already in one.

STIMULUS PLAN

Indeed, each day the government seemed to report more bleak news about the economy. In early January, the U.S. Labor Department reported that the nation's unemployment rate hit 5 percent, meaning that 1 in 20 Americans was now out of work. It was the highest unemployment rate in two years. In fact, during December the Labor Department said American companies had cut a total of 13,000 jobs. "The economy is getting hit by some body blows," economist Ken Mayland said. "The big question is whether the economy can withstand it or will it take a fall?"[3]

A few days later, the Labor Department reported some more bad news: The inflation rate in the United States for 2007 was the highest in 17 years. The department reported that prices for consumer goods such as food, gasoline, and clothing, rose by 4.1 percent, nearly double the increase recorded in 2006. Meanwhile, the department reported, people's wages failed to keep up with the rising cost of goods—during 2007, average weekly earnings actually *dropped* by nearly 1 percent. It meant that during 2007, people had less money to buy goods and services that cost more than they ever did before. Since consumer spending fuels some 70 percent of the economic activity in the United States, any drop in the buying power of Americans is sure to have a disastrous effect on the economy.

Clearly, Pelosi as well as Senate Majority Leader Harry Reid knew the problem had to be addressed quickly. What's more, the political consequences of failing to rescue the economy could be significant. For starters, President Bush was beginning his final year in office. He did not want to leave a legacy of economic ruin. Republicans on Capitol Hill were also anxious for a stimulus plan to pass—they feared they would bear the brunt of voter backlash should the economy fall further into a tailspin. Meanwhile, the 2008 campaign for the presidency had been under way for some months. The economy had already surfaced as a major issue in the campaign. Each of the major candidates proposed their own solutions for the ailing economy. At

WOMEN OF THE HOUSE

When Nancy Pelosi accepted the gavel as speaker of the U.S. House, she was one of 29 women who presided over the world's national legislatures, of which there are 188. By 2007, women were presiding over parliaments and similar lawmaking bodies in countries as diverse as Albania, Israel, the Gambia, Venezuela, the Bahamas, Turkmenistan, and New Zealand.

The first country to elect a woman to preside over a legislative body was Austria, where Olga Rudel-Zeynek served as president of the parliament, which is known as the *Bundesrat*, in 1927, 1928, and 1932. In fact, Rudel-Zeynek was the only woman known to have led a legislature before World War II.

Following the war, women made great strides in achieving representation in the world's lawmaking bodies, but a 2006 analysis by the Inter-Parliamentary Union, an agency of the United Nations, found that women were still underrepresented in national legislatures. The study found that, while women make up roughly half the world's population, no legislature features a membership that is half female. In the Nordic countries of Sweden, Denmark, Norway, and Finland, women compose about 40 percent of the membership of the legislatures, while in the Arab states, female representation in national legislatures is as low as 8 percent. (In the U.S. Congress, in 2007, women made up the White House as well as on Capitol Hill, Democrats and Republicans knew they would have to forge a plan, but in the volatile election year of 2008, neither side wanted to give in to the other's demands.

Nevertheless, amid all this uncertainty and suspicion, by mid-January meetings among the key participants had

about 16 percent of the membership of both chambers—in the House, 71 of 435 members were women, while in the Senate, 16 of 100 members were women.)

Female participation in the lawmaking bodies of Arab states is often low because many Arab states are guided by Islamic law and custom, which often do not recognize full citizenship rights for women. On the other hand, some Islamic countries maintain a much broader interpretation of Islamic law. Pakistan, for example, is one of the most politically volatile nations in the world, yet women have enjoyed a major influence over the government. Before her assassination in late 2007, Benazir Bhutto twice served as prime minister. Later in 2008, Pakistan's legislature elected its first female speaker, Fehmida Mirza, a longtime ally of Bhutto's. An opposition legislator, Tariq Azim, said he believed that Mirza could provide a calming influence on the often incendiary tempers that flare in the country's legislature. "The house will be more disciplined and better managed," he said, "as you know there is more respect for a woman in our country."*

*Stephen Graham, Associated Press. "Pakistan Chooses Female Parliament Speaker." *The Philadelphia Inquirer*, March 20, 2008, p. A-4.

commenced. The first meeting occurred in Pelosi's office on Capitol Hill, where Benjamin Bernanke, chairman of the Federal Reserve Board—which regulates the American banking system—recommended an economic-stimulus package that would provide cash payments to Americans. Essentially, Bernanke recommended that Congress authorize the Treasury Department to send each American a lump sum that, theoretically, people would spend for goods and services in the economy. By making that cash available to Americans, Bernanke argued, they would in turn pump billions of dollars into the economy, spurring businesses to sell more goods and create more jobs. A similar but smaller program had been enacted during a brief recession in 2001. To address the stagnant economy that year, Congress cut the tax rates paid by most Americans. Since Americans had already paid their taxes for 2001, Congress directed that tax-rebate checks be sent to all taxpayers. Most Americans received payments of $300.

There is no question that, as the bleak economic picture of 2008 unfolded, most Americans needed something more than $300 to help make ends meet. As Pelosi met with Bernanke, President Bush had also decided that rebates would have to be a part of an economic-stimulus plan. At the White House, he directed his chief economic aides to draft a plan to provide rebates to Americans.

TENSE CONFERENCE CALL

Bush wanted the plan to include more than just payments to economically stressed Americans. In 2001 and 2003, he pushed through Congress a series of tax breaks, which have been perceived mostly to aid businesses, arguing that businesses prosper most when their tax burden is reduced. Those tax cuts are due to expire in 2010. As part of the stimulus plan, Bush wanted the cuts made permanent.

Democrats balked at that demand, mostly because the Bush tax cuts also slashed rates that people pay on investment returns, a circumstance that mostly benefits wealthy Americans. Early in the negotiations, Reid and Pelosi made it clear to the president that they would not support an extension of his tax cuts.

Still, negotiations moved quickly. It appeared the two sides were close to drafting a package when Bush suddenly suggested that he would unfurl his own plan, which would likely not include aid for taxpayers in the lowest income brackets. During a tense conference call on January 17, Pelosi and Reid warned the president against proposing his own plan. The call ended with both sides fuming. A few minutes later, Bush told Paulson to call Pelosi and Reid and say he would drop plans to devise his own stimulus package. "That's when we really got the feeling from the White House side that things would really be different," said New York Senator Charles Schumer, who participated in the negotiations. "It bought a lot of good will."[4]

At 7 A.M. on January 23, Paulson as well as congressional leaders from both parties met at the Capitol. After serving doughnuts and fruit cups, Pelosi laid out her demands: The package would have to extend to all Americans, not just taxpayers. She wanted to ensure that unemployed people or people who earn less than $3,000 a year—and, therefore, do not pay taxes—would share in the rebates. In addition, she demanded more funding for unemployment benefits and food stamps, which are assistance programs for the nation's neediest people.

The Republicans in the meeting balked at the demands, arguing that low-income people would have little impact on stimulating the economy. John Boehner, the House minority leader, insisted that the stimulus package be aimed mostly at middle-class taxpayers. "Philosophically, as Republicans, (we say) all people who pay taxes ought to get relief," Boehner said later. "We wanted to get money back to middle-class families as efficiently as possible."[5]

The meeting broke up without an agreement, but the two sides planned to reconvene later in the day. At 2 P.M., the participants met again in Pelosi's office. This time, Boehner shocked the Democrats by announcing that Republicans would support most of Pelosi's plan for aiding low-income people. Boehner said the Republicans in Congress would agree to provide rebate checks to low-income Americans, but the GOP would not support expanding food stamps and unemployment compensation. Reluctantly, the Democrats agreed to the compromise. "Life is a series of trade-offs,"[6] shrugged Illinois Representative Rahm Emanuel, who participated in the negotiations.

OPPOSITION IN THE DEMOCRATIC CAUCUS

Not all members of the Democratic caucus were willing to agree to drop increases in food stamps and unemployment compensation from the final package. Representative Charles B. Rangel, a New York Democrat and chairman of the powerful House Ways and Means Committee—a panel that would have to sign off on the legislation—told Pelosi he would oppose it unless those programs were given a boost in the package. "You can bet your life that there will be increases in the amounts of moneys for unemployment compensation [and] there will be money for food stamps,"[7] Rangel insisted to reporters.

Pelosi and Rangel met for several hours. The meeting ended with the speaker persuading Rangel to accept the package that had been negotiated with the Republicans. She promised that the House would consider legislation later in the year to increase assistance to the neediest Americans. Rangel accepted her promise but said he was still troubled by leaving some Americans out of the stimulus package. Said Rangel, "(Americans) will spend the rebate to put food on their tables, shoes on their kids' feet, and roofs over their heads, yet I caution my colleagues against walking out of this House with pride on passage of this bill because there are too many families who find themselves in this predicament."[8]

On January 24—less than two weeks after Pelosi had her first meeting with Bernanke—congressional leaders announced they had agreed on a $150 billion stimulus package. The centerpiece of the package was a tax rebate to every American taxpayer—by the middle of the year, most working couples would receive $1,200 or more while individuals would receive $600. It was hoped that the infusion of cash into the pockets of taxpayers would prompt them to spend the money, helping to spur the growth of businesses.

The tax rebates added up to $100 billion. At President Bush's insistence, another $50 billion was added to the plan, giving tax incentives to businesses to invest in new manufacturing facilities as well as equipment. As Pelosi demanded, Bush and the Republicans on Capitol Hill agreed that nontaxpayers would receive payments of $300 each. Also as expected, there was no increase in benefits for the recipients of food stamps or unemployment compensation. "I can't say I'm totally pleased with the package, but I do know it will help stimulate the economy," Pelosi said. "But if it does not, then there will be more to come."[9]

Still, when the stimulus package was adopted by Congress, critics believed that Bush agreed to much more aid to middle- and lower-income people than he originally wanted, and that the legislation bore the thumbprint of Pelosi more than anybody else who participated in the negotiations. "I could put a bill on the table any day," Pelosi said after the package was adopted. "So I had that kind of leverage. We all knew we had to do something for the American people. The question was what?"[10]

Nancy Pelosi appeared at an event in April 2008 to mark the beginning of the delivery of economic-stimulus checks to the American people. The passage of the economic-stimulus legislation came together in a matter of a few weeks in early 2008.

A few weeks later, the measure passed both houses of Congress with broad bipartisan support: It passed the Senate by a margin of 81 to 16, while the House adopted the plan by a vote of 380 to 34. By early May, the Treasury Department started to issue rebate payments to Americans. Adoption of the economic-stimulus plan had taken just a few weeks. It showed that Washington could react quickly to a crisis. Wrote the *Wall Street Journal*, "It was a rare display of compromise and speed in a city known recently for partisan gridlock."[11]

LOOKING TO THE FUTURE

As Nancy Pelosi looks back on her first years as speaker, it is clear that she has avoided a strictly partisan agenda as she guided the House of Representatives through some of the nation's most turbulent issues. What's more, she has managed to fashion an agenda of reform, economic stimulus, and progressive energy initiatives during an era when the opposing party has occupied the White House. Looking to the future, Pelosi and other Democratic leaders wonder what they can accomplish with a member of their party occupying the White House.

In the meantime, she has etched her place in history as a defender of some of the most oppressed people in America and the world, but she has also indicated a willingness to compromise with her opponents to achieve her goals. As the first woman to hold the position of speaker of the House, one of the most powerful jobs in government, there is no question that Pelosi has broken through the marble ceiling, opening the way for other women to break through as well. Says Pelosi:

> If I have one piece of advice for women who want to get involved and make a difference, it is this: Just run. Run for student government, run for local office, run for higher office. Anything is possible for women in our country. The marble ceiling in Congress has been shattered. Having a woman as speaker sends a message to young girls and women across the country that anything is possible for them, that women can achieve power, wield power, and breathe the air at that altitude. As the first woman speaker of the House, I know that I will not be the last.[12]

CHRONOLOGY

1940 Nancy Patricia D'Alesandro is born on March 26 in Baltimore, Maryland.

1954 Enrolls in the Institute of Notre Dame, a private Catholic girls school in Baltimore.

1957 Meets Massachusetts Senator John F. Kennedy at a dinner in Baltimore; three years later, she campaigns for Kennedy when he runs for the presidency.

1958 Graduates from the Institute of Notre Dame and enrolls in Trinity College in Washington, D.C.

1962 Graduates from Trinity College.

1963 Paul and Nancy Pelosi marry and move to New York City.

1969 The Pelosis move to San Francisco, California, where Nancy becomes active in local Democratic politics.

1976 Returns to Maryland to run the presidential campaign for California Governor Jerry Brown in the Maryland primary, delivering an upset victory for Brown.

1984 Uses her influence as chairwoman of the California State Democratic Committee to stage the party's national convention in San Francisco.

1987 Wins a special election to replace Sala Burton, representing a district in Northern California in the U.S. House.

1990 Defies American Catholic leaders by maintaining her support for abortion rights.

1991 Votes against authorizing force to repel Iraqi invaders from Kuwait and leads a protest against the Chinese government in Tiananmen Square in Beijing.

1992 Following the confirmation hearings of U.S. Supreme Court Justice Clarence Thomas, in which a former aide alleged that Thomas had sexually harassed her, 24 new female members of the House and five new female members of the Senate are elected.

2001 Pelosi is elected House Democratic whip, the second-highest position in the Democratic caucus; airliners hijacked by terrorists crash into the World Trade Center in New York, the Pentagon in Washington, and a field in Pennsylvania, killing some 3,000 people.

2002 Pelosi is elected House minority leader, at the time the highest position in her party's caucus; votes against providing President Bush with the authorization to invade Iraq.

2003 Backed by overwhelming public support at home, American forces invade Iraq and oust dictator Saddam Hussein.

2004 As casualties increase and abuses are reported at the Abu Ghraib military prison, public opinion begins to turn against the war in Iraq.

2006 Responding to Republican scandals in Congress and displaying a weariness for the war in Iraq, voters elect a Democratic majority in the House and the Senate for the first time in a dozen years, clearing the way for Pelosi to be elected House speaker.

2007 On January 4, Pelosi is elected speaker of the U.S. House; initiates her Hundred Hours agenda but fails to set deadlines for troop withdrawals from Iraq.

2008 Helps to engineer an economic-stimulus plan that includes $150 billion in cash assistance for taxpayers, low-income people, and businesses.

NOTES

CHAPTER 1: MADAM SPEAKER

1. Kate Zernike. "A Shift in Power, Starting with 'Madam Speaker.'" *The New York Times*, January 24, 2007, p. A-1.
2. Ibid.
3. Ibid.
4. Emily Goodin. "Speaking of Women." *National Journal*. Vol. 39 (Jan. 6, 2007): p. 56.
5. John M. Broder. "Jubilant Democrats Assume Control on Capitol Hill." *The New York Times*, January 5, 2007, p. A-1.
6. Nancy Pelosi. "Text of Nancy Pelosi's Speech." *San Francisco Chronicle*, January 4, 2007: Available online at http://sfgate.com/cgi-bin/article.cgi?f=/c/a/2007/01/04/BAG5ANCTQ27.DTL.
7. Terence Hunt, Associated Press. "Bush Stands Firm on War." *Albany Times Union*, January 24, 2007, p. A-1.
8. Ibid.

CHAPTER 2: BORN INTO POLITICS

1. John Powers. "House Proud." *Vogue*. Vol. 197 (March 2007): p. 557.
2. Mary Ann Cooper. "All I Hoped It Would Be." *Grand*. Vol. 3 (July-August 2007): p. 45.
3. Vincent Bzdek. *Woman of the House: The Rise of Nancy Pelosi*. New York: Palgrave Macmillan, 2008, p. 31.
4. Ellen Gamerman. "Child of Politics, All Grown Up." *Baltimore Sun*, November 14, 2002, p. 1-A.
5. *Scarborough Country*, January 22, 2007. Available online at http://www.msnbc.msn.com/id/16771757/.
6. Gamerman, "Child of Politics, All Grown Up."
7. Johanna Neuman. "Hard Work, Political Roots Fuel Pelosi's Rise." *Los Angeles Times*, November 10, 2002, p. A-1.
8. Ben A. Franklin. "Brown's Victory Sets Back Georgian's Presidency Bid." *The New York Times*, May 19, 1976, p. 47.
9. Edward Epstein. "Pelosi: Lifetime Commitment to Politics, Democrats." *San Francisco Chronicle*, November 8, 2006, p. A-11.

CHAPTER 3: RISE TO THE TOP

1. P.J. Corkery. "Gore Looking for Work in Silli Valley." *San Francisco Examiner*, March 26, 2001.
2. Chris Bull. "California's 5th District Seat to Go to Pelosi; Britt Loses Race, But Wins Gay Leftist Vote." *Gay Community News*. Vol. 14 (April 12-18, 1987): p. 1.
3. Val Muchowski. "Nancy Pelosi," National Women's Political Caucus of California. (November 2002).

4. Mark McNamara. "Gay Candidate: Judge Record, Not Lifestyle." *USA Today*, April 7, 1987, p. 2-A.
5. Bzdek, *Woman of the House*, p. 93.
6. Bill Ghent. "A Leader on Our Side." *The Advocate*, December 24, 2002. Available online at http://www.advocate.com/html/stories/879/879_pelosi.asp.
7. Nancy Pelosi. "House Vote to Increase NEA and NEH Funding a Victory of Imagination Over Ideology." Congresswoman Nancy Pelosi news release (July 17, 2002). Available online at http://www.house.gov/pelosi/prNEAandNEHFunding071702.htm.
8. Robin Toner. "Catholic Politicians Confront Public and Private Conscience." *The New York Times*, June 25, 1990, p. A-1.
9. Bzdek, *Woman of the House*, p. 100.
10. Ibid., p. 134.
11. Ibid., p. 135.

CHAPTER 4: THE HUNDRED HOURS AGENDA

1. Jim Abrams. "House Approves Outside Ethics Panel." Associated Press, March 11, 2008. Available online at http://ap.google.com/article/ALeqM5jSM0eJMgSJ3Gi549o4LSMmk5bOwwD8VBKC6G8.
2. Matt Kelley. "House OKs Independent Ethics Board." *USA Today*, March 14, 2008, p. A-6.
3. Lyndsey Layton. "Culture Shock on Capitol Hill: House to Work Five Days a Week." *The Washington Post*, December 6, 2006, p. A-1.
4. Ibid.
5. David Espo, Associated Press. "Minimum Wage Wins in House; Democrats in Senate Are Ready to Deal with Bush to Make $7.25 a Reality." *Albany Times Union*, January 11, 2007, p. A-4.
6. Ibid.
7. Bruce Japsen. "Fight Seen as House OKs Drug Price Bill; Senate Fate Uncertain; Bush Veto Seen Likely." *Chicago Tribune*, January 13, 2007, p. 1.
8. Nancy Pelosi. "Requiring Medicare Prescription Drug Negotiations Is a Resounding Victory for America's Seniors." Speaker Nancy Pelosi news release. (January. 12, 2007). Available online at http://speaker.house.gov/newsroom/pressreleases?id=0031.
9. Jeff Zeleny. "House Votes to Expand Stem Cell Research." *The New York Times*, June 8, 2007, p. A-24.
10. Ibid.
11. David Greene. "Bush Vetoes Bill to Expand Stem Cell Research." National Public Radio, July 19, 2006. Available

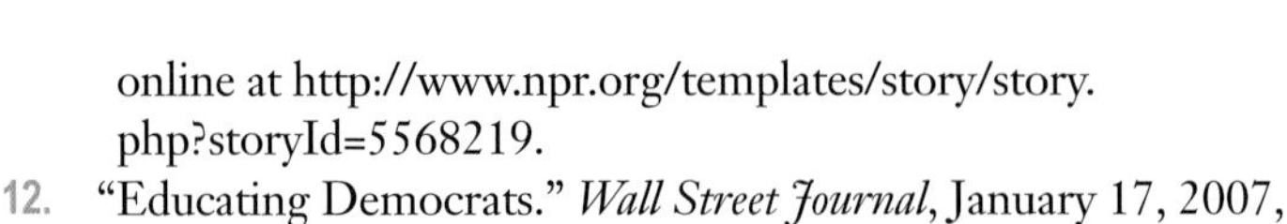

online at http://www.npr.org/templates/story/story.php?storyId=5568219.

12. "Educating Democrats." *Wall Street Journal*, January 17, 2007, p. A-18.
13. Carl Hulse. "After 42 Hours (Or So), House Democrats Complete 100-Hour Push." *The New York Times*, January 19, 2007, p. A-19.

CHAPTER 5: THAWING THE MIDDLE EAST ICE

1. Michael McAuliff. "Hit and Miss for Speaker of the House Pelosi: 100 Day Report Card." *New York Daily News*, April 8, 2007, p. 22.
2. Ibid.
3. Hassan M. Fattah. "Pelosi, Warmly Greeted in Syria, Is Criticized by White House." *The New York Times*, April 4, 2007, p. A-6.
4. Robert F. Turner. "Illegal Diplomacy." *Wall Street Journal*, April 6, 2007, p. A-10.
5. Michael Abramowitz and Lois Romano. "Differing Tales of a White House Encounter." *The Washington Post*, April 20, 2007, p. A-29.
6. Trudy Rubin. "Why Criticize Pelosi for Bush Mess? Sure, Her Visit to Syria Will Do Nothing Except Possibly Boost Assad, but the Mideast Morass Is the White House's Fault." *The Philadelphia Inquirer*, April 8, 2007, p. D-1.
7. Nancy Pelosi. "Pelosi Address to Israeli Knesset." April 1, 2007. Available online at http://speaker.house.gov/newsroom/speeches?id=0031.
8. Fattah. "Pelosi, Warmly Greeted in Syria, Is Criticized by White House."
9. Yoav Stern. "U.S. Republican Meets Assad Day After Contentious Pelosi Visit." *Haaretz*, April 7, 2007. Available online at http://www.haaretz.com/hasen/spages/845904.html.
10. "Pratfall in Damascus." *The Washington Post*, April 5, 2007, p. A-16.
11. Ibid.
12. Newt Gingrich. "Nancy Pelosi: The Lady of the House Takes Charge." *Time*. Vol. 169 (May 14, 2007): p. 59.
13. Hassan M. Fattah. "Pelosi's Delegation Presses Syrian Leader on Militants." *The New York Times*, April 5, 2007, p. A-3.
14. Donna Abu-Nasr, Associated Press. "Pelosi Visits Saudi Arabia's Council." *The Washington Post*, April 6, 2007, p. A-18.
15. Steven Erlanger. "Syria Plans to Attend Meeting on Mideast Peace." *The New York Times*, November 26, 2007, p. A-1.

CHAPTER 6: OPPOSING THE WAR

1. Bryan Bender. "Rumsfeld Will Stay, President Insists; Democrats Intensify Calls for Resignation." *Boston Globe*, May 7, 2004, p. A-1.
2. Edward Epstein. "Bush Gets Power to Strike Iraq." *San Francisco Chronicle*, October 11, 2002, p. A-1.
3. "Bush: Several Factors Determined Vote." United Press International, November 8, 2006. Available online at http://www.upi.com/NewsTrack/Top_News/2006/11/08/bush_several_factors_determined_vote/5278/.
4. Michael Abramowitz and Jonathan Weisman. "Bush Meets with Pelosi; Both Vow Cooperation." *The Washington Post*, November 10, 2006, p. A-1.
5. Bzdek. *Woman of the House*, p. 216.
6. Ibid., p. 220.
7. Associated Press. "Cindy Sheehan May Run Against House Speaker Nancy Pelosi in 2008." Fox News, July 9, 2007. Available online at http://www.foxnews.com/story/0,2933,288589,00.html.
8. Bzdek. *Woman of the House*, p. 223.
9. Carl Hulse. "Democrats Pull Troop Deadline from Iraq Bill." *The New York Times*, May 23, 2007, p. A-1.

CHAPTER 7: "IMPEACHMENT IS OFF THE TABLE"

1. Thomas Ferraro. "Pelosi Greeted with 'Impeach' Bush and Cheney Buttons." Reuters, January 18, 2008. Available online at http://blogs.reuters.com/trail08/2008/01/18/pelosi-greeted-with-impeach-bush-and-cheney-buttons.
2. Elizabeth Holtzman. "Judiciary Committee Should Move to Impeach Bush and Cheney." *The Philadelphia Inquirer*, January 27, 2008, p. D-6.
3. U.S. Constitution, Article II, Section 4.
4. *Bill Moyers Journal*. PBS, July 13. 2007. Available online at http://www.pbs.org/moyers/journal/07132007/transcript2.html.
5. "New Poll: Majority of Americans Support Impeachment." AfterDowningStreet.org news release, November 4, 2005. Available online at http://www.afterdowningstreet.org/?q=node/4421.
6. David Freddoso. "Pelosi Punts—for Now—on Impeachment." *Human Events*. Vol. 62 (March 20, 2006): p. 1.
7. Edward Epstein. "A Democrat-Controlled House Wouldn't Impeach, Pelosi Says." *San Francisco Chronicle*, May 13, 2006, p. A-1.
8. Ibid.

9. "Nancy Pelosi: Two Heartbeats Away." CBS News, October 20, 2006. Available online at http://www.cbsnews.com/stories/2006/10/20/60minutes/main2111089.shtml.
10. Epstein. "A Democrat-Controlled House Wouldn't Impeach, Pelosi Says."
11. *Bill Moyers Journal*. PBS, July 13, 2007.
12. Michael Tomasky. "A Trial Would Fail, and Split the U.S. When Unity Behind Progressive Ideas Is Needed." *The Philadelphia Inquirer*, January 27, 2008, p. D-1.
13. John Curran, Associated Press. "Two Vermont Towns Approve Bush-Cheney Indictment Articles." *Boston Globe*, March 4, 2008. Available online at http://www.boston.com/news/local/vermont/articles/2008/03/04/in_brattleboro_bush_cheney_indictment_on_ballot.
14. Ferraro. "Pelosi Greeted with 'Impeach' Bush and Cheney Buttons."

CHAPTER 8: BREAKING THROUGH THE GRIDLOCK

1. Erica Werner. "Iraq War Losses Cloud Speaker's Year." Associated Press, January 1, 2008. Available online at http://ap.google.com/article/ALeqM5iXRurPqiJaRNLxY3-Rj9wWgVH1vwD8TSV1880.
2. Mark Memmott and Jill Lawrence. "Gallup: Approval Rating for Congress Matches Lowest Ever Recorded." *USA Today*, August 21, 2007. Available online at http://blogs.usatoday.com/onpolitics/2007/08/gallup-approval.html.
3. Carl Hulse and Robert Pear. "Republican Unity Trumps Democratic Momentum." *The New York Times*, December 21, 2007, p. A-36.
4. Robert Pear. "House Defies Bush and Passes Children's Insurance Bill." *The New York Times*, October 26, 2007, p. A-19.
5. Robert Pear. "House Passes Children's Insurance Measure." *The New York Times*, September 26, 2007, p. A-25.
6. Janet Hook. "President May Be Limping, but He's Yet to be a Lame Duck." *The Philadelphia Inquirer*, December 23, 2007, p. A-14.
7. Edmund L. Andrews. "Veteran Democratic Bulldog Guards House Turf on Energy." *The New York Times*, July 21, 2007, p. A-1.
8. John Donnelly. "Gore Takes His Global-Warming Battle to Congress; Calls for Taxing Big Polluters, Emission Freeze." *Boston Globe*, March 22, 2007, p. A-13.
9. Richard Simon. "Cloud Over Corn's Moment in Sun; An Ethanol Mandate, Popular in Farm States, Is Seen as Key to Passing an Energy Bill." *Los Angeles Times*, November 28, 2007, p. A-18.

10. Neil Modie. “Pelosi Brings Promise to Seattle to Keep Energy Dollars at Home.” *Seattle Post-Intelligencer*, April 13, 2007. Available online at http://seattlepi.nwsource.com/local/311623_pelosi14.html.
11. Richard Simon. “House Passes a Sweeping Energy Bill.” *Los Angeles Times*, December 7, 2007, p. A-17.
12. Nancy Pelosi. “Energy Bill Will Be ‘Shot Heard Round the World’ for Energy Independence.” Reuters, December 6, 2007. Available online at http://www.reuters.com/article/pressRelease/idUS21743+07-Dec-2007+PRN20071207.

CHAPTER 9: RESCUING THE ECONOMY

1. Carl Hulse. “For Speaker, Calculated Stimulus Steps.” *The New York Times*, January 27, 2008, p. A-19.
2. Michael M. Phillips, Sarah Lueck, and Sudeep Reddy. “Stimulus Deal Spurred by Fears of Voter Backlash.” *Wall Street Journal*, January 26–27, 2008, p. A-6.
3. Associated Press. “National Unemployment Rate Hits 5 Percent.” *New York Daily News*, January 4, 2008. Available online at http://www.nydailynews.com/money/2008/01/04/2008-01-04_national_unemployment_rate_hits_5_percen.html.
4. Phillips, Lueck, and Reddy. “Stimulus Deal Spurred by Fears of Voter Backlash.”
5. Sarah Lueck, Timothy Aeppel, and Michael M. Phillips. “Washington Sets $150 Billion Plan to Jolt Economy.” *Wall Street Journal*, January 25, 2008, p. A-8.
6. Phillips, Lueck, and Reddy. “Stimulus Deal Spurred by Fears of Voter Backlash.”
7. Kenneth R. Bazinet. “Dems Talk Up Quick Job on Econ Package.” *New York Daily News*, January 21, 2008, p. 6.
8. Kenneth R. Bazinet. “Econ Stimulus Plan Moves to Senate.” *New York Daily News*, January 30, 2008, p. 10.
9. Susan Page and Richard Wolf. “$150 Billion ‘Insurance Policy’ Aimed at Shaky Economy.” *USA Today*, January 25, 2008, p. 4-A.
10. Hulse. “For Speaker, Calculated Stimulus Steps.”
11. Lueck, Aeppel and Phillips. “Washington Sets $150 Billion Plan to Jolt Economy.”
12. Cooper. “All I Hoped It Would Be.”

BIBLIOGRAPHY

Abramowitz, Michael, and Lois Romano. "Differing Tales of a White House Encounter." *Washington Post*, April 20, 2007, p. A-29.

Abramowitz, Michael, and Jonathan Weisman. "Bush Meets with Pelosi; Both Vow Cooperation." *Washington Post*, November 10, 2006, p. A-1.

Abrams, Jim. "House Approves Outside Ethics Panel." Associated Press, March 11, 2008. Available online at http://ap.google.com/article/ALeqM5jSM0eJMgSJ3Gi549o4LSMmk5bOwwD8VBKC6G8.

Abu-Nasr, Donna, Associated Press. "Pelosi Visits Saudi Arabia's Council." *Washington Post*, April 6, 2007, p. A-18.

Andrews, Edmund L. "Veteran Democratic Bulldog Guards House Turf on Energy." *New York Times*, July 21, 2007, p. A-1.

Associated Press. "Cindy Sheehan May Run Against House Speaker Nancy Pelosi in 2008." Fox News, July 9, 2007. Available online at http://www.foxnews.com/story/0,2933,288589,00.html.

Associated Press. "National Unemployment Rate Hits 5 Percent." *New York Daily News*, January 4, 2008. Available online at http://www.nydailynews.com/money/2008/01/04/2008-01-04_national_unemployment_rate_hits_5_percen.html.

Bazinet, Kenneth R. "Dems Talk Up Quick Job on Econ Package." *New York Daily News*, January 21, 2008, p. 6.

———. "Econ Stimulus Plan Moves to Senate." *New York Daily News*, January 30, 2008, p. 10.

Bender, Bryan. "Rumsfeld Will Stay, President Insists; Democrats Intensify Calls for Resignation." *Boston Globe*, May 7, 2004, p. A-1.

Bill Moyers Journal. PBS, July 13. 2007. Available online at http://www.pbs.org/moyers/journal/07132007/transcript2.html.

Broder, John M. "Jubilant Democrats Assume Control on Capitol Hill." *New York Times*, January 5, 2007, p. A-1.

Bull, Chris. "California's 5th District Seat to Go to Pelosi; Britt Loses Race, But Wins Gay Leftist Vote." *Gay Community News*. Vol. 14 (April 12-18, 1987): p. 1.

"Bush: Several Factors Determined Vote." United Press International, November 8, 2006. Available online at http://www.upi.com/NewsTrack/Top_News/2006/11/08/bush_several_factors_determined_vote/5278/.

Bzdek, Vincent. *Woman of the House: The Rise of Nancy Pelosi*. New York: Palgrave Macmillan, 2008.

Clift, Eleanor, and Tom Brazaitis. *Madam President: Women Blazing the Leadership Trail*. New York: Routlege, 2003.

Cooper, Mary Ann. "All I Hoped It Would Be." *Grand*. Vol. 3 (July-August 2007): pp. 45-46.

Corkery, P.J. "Gore Looking for Work in Silli Valley." *San Francisco Examiner*, March 26, 2001.

Curran, John, Associated Press. "Two Vermont Towns Approve Bush-Cheney Indictment Articles." *Boston Globe*, March 4, 2008. Available online at http://www.boston.com/news/local/vermont/articles/2008/03/04/in_brattleboro_bush_cheney_indictment_on_ballot.

Donnelly, John. "Gore Takes His Global-Warming Battle to Congress; Calls for Taxing Big Polluters, Emission Freeze." *Boston Globe*, March 22, 2007, p. A-13.

"Educating Democrats." *Wall Street Journal*, January 17, 2007, p. A-18.

Epstein, Edward. "Bush Gets Power to Strike Iraq." *San Francisco Chronicle*, October 11, 2002, p. A-1.

———. "A Democrat-Controlled House Wouldn't Impeach, Pelosi Says." *San Francisco Chronicle*, May 13, 2006, p. A-1.

———. "Pelosi: Lifetime Commitment to Politics, Democrats." *San Francisco Chronicle*, November 8, 2006, p. A-11.

Erlanger, Steven. "Syria Plans to Attend Meeting on Mideast Peace," *New York Times*, November 26, 2007, p. A-1.

Espo, David, Associated Press. "Minimum Wage Wins in House; Democrats in Senate Are Ready to Deal with Bush to Make $7.25 a Reality." *Albany Times Union*, January 11, 2007, p. A-4.

Fattah, Hassan M. "Pelosi, Warmly Greeted in Syria, Is Criticized by White House." *New York Times*, April 4, 2007, p. A-6.

———. "Pelosi's Delegation Presses Syrian Leader on Militants." *New York Times*, April 5, 2007, p. A-3.

Ferraro, Thomas. "Pelosi Greeted with 'Impeach' Bush and Cheney Buttons." Reuters, January 18, 2008. Available online at http://blogs.reuters.com/trail08/2008/01/18/pelosi-greeted-with-impeach-bush-and-cheney-buttons.

Fields-Meyer, Thomas. "Lady of the House." *People*. Vol. 66 (Dec. 18, 2006): p. 81.

Franklin, Ben A. "Brown's Victory Sets Back Georgian's Presidency Bid." *New York Times*, May 19, 1976, p. 47.

Freddoso, David. "Pelosi Punts—for Now—on Impeachment." *Human Events*. Vol. 62 (March 20, 2006): p. 1.

Gamerman, Ellen. "Child of Politics, All Grown Up." *Baltimore Sun*, November 14, 2002, p. 1-A.

Ghent, Bill. "A Leader on Our Side." *The Advocate*, December 24, 2002. Available online at http://www.advocate.com/html/stories/879/879_pelosi.asp.

Gingrich, Newt. "Nancy Pelosi: The Lady of the House Takes Charge." *Time*. Vol. 169 (May 14, 2007): p. 59.

Goodin, Emily. "Speaking of Women." *National Journal*. Vol. 39 (Jan. 6, 2007): p. 56.

Graham, Stephen, Associated Press. "Pakistan Chooses Female Parliament Speaker." *Philadelphia Inquirer*, March 20, 2008, p. A-4.

Greene, David. "Bush Vetoes Bill to Expand Stem Cell Research." National Public Radio, July 19, 2006. Available online at http://www.npr.org/templates/story/story.php?storyId=5568219.

Holtzman, Elizabeth. "Judiciary Committee Should Move to Impeach Bush and Cheney." *Philadelphia Inquirer*, January 27, 2008, p. D-6.

Hook, Janet. "President May Be Limping, but He's Yet to be a Lame Duck." *Philadelphia Inquirer*, December 23, 2007, p. A-14.

Hulse, Carl. "After 42 Hours (Or So), House Democrats Complete 100-Hour Push." *New York Times*, January 19, 2007, p. A-19.

———. "Democrats Pull Troop Deadline from Iraq Bill." *New York Times*, May 23, 2007, p. A-1.

———. "For Speaker, Calculated Stimulus Steps." *New York Times*, January 27, 2008, p. A-19.

Hulse, Carl, and Robert Pear. "Republican Unity Trumps Democratic Momentum." *New York Times*, December 21, 2007, p. A-36.

Hunt, Terence, Associated Press. "Bush Stands Firm on War." *Albany Times Union*, January 24, 2007, p. A-1.

Japsen, Bruce. "Fight Seen as House OKs Drug Price Bill; Senate Fate Uncertain; Bush Veto Seen Likely." *Chicago Tribune*, January 13, 2007, p. 1.

Kelley, Matt. "House OKs Independent Ethics Board." *USA Today*, March 14, 2008, p. A-6.

Layton, Lyndsey. "Culture Shock on Capitol Hill: House to Work Five Days a Week." *Washington Post*, December 6, 2006, p. A-1.

Lueck, Sarah, Timothy Aeppel, and Michael M. Phillips. "Washington Sets $150 Billion Plan to Jolt Economy." *Wall Street Journal*, January 25, 2008, p. A-8.

Memmott, Mark, and Jill Lawrence. "Gallup: Approval Rating for Congress Matches Lowest Ever Recorded." *USA Today*, August 21, 2007. Available online at http://blogs.usatoday.com/onpolitics/2007/08/gallup-approval.html.

McAuliff, Michael. "Hit and Miss for Speaker of the House Pelosi: 100 Day Report Card." *New York Daily News*, April 8, 2007, p. 22.

McNamara, Mark. "Gay Candidate: Judge Record, Not Lifestyle." *USA Today*, April 7, 1987, p. 2-A.

Modie, Neil. "Pelosi Brings Promise to Seattle to Keep Energy Dollars at Home." *Seattle Post-Intelligencer*, April 13, 2007. Available online at http://seattlepi.nwsource.com/local/311623_pelosi14.html.

Muchowski, Val. "Nancy Pelosi," National Women's Political Caucus of California. (November 2002).

"Nancy Pelosi: Two Heartbeats Away." CBS News, October 20, 2006. Available online at http://www.cbsnews.com/stories/2006/10/20/60minutes/main2111089.shtml.

Neuman, Johanna. "Hard Work, Political Roots Fuel Pelosi's Rise." *Los Angeles Times*, November 10, 2002, p. A-1.

"New Poll: Majority of Americans Support Impeachment." AfterDowningStreet.org news release, November 4, 2005. Available online at http://www.afterdowningstreet.org/?q=node/4421.

Page, Susan, and Richard Wolf. "$150 Billion 'Insurance Policy' Aimed at Shaky Economy." *USA Today*, January 25, 2008, p. 4-A.

Pear, Robert. "House Defies Bush and Passes Children's Insurance Bill." *New York Times*, October 26, 2007, p. A-19.

———. "House Passes Children's Insurance Measure." *New York Times*, September 26, 2007, p. A-25.

Pelosi, Nancy. "Energy Bill Will Be 'Shot Heard Round the World' for Energy Independence." Reuters, December 6, 2007. Available online at http://www.reuters.com/article/pressRelease/idUS21743+07-Dec-2007+PRN20071207.

———. "House Vote to Increase NEA and NEH Funding a Victory of Imagination Over Ideology." Congresswoman Nancy Pelosi news release (July 17, 2002). Available online at http://www.house.gov/pelosi/prNEAandNEHFunding071702.htm.

———. "Pelosi Address to Israeli Knesset." April 1, 2007. Available online at http://speaker.house.gov/newsroom/speeches?id=0031.

———. "Requiring Medicare Prescription Drug Negotiations Is a Resounding Victory for America's Seniors." Speaker Nancy Pelosi news release. (January. 12, 2007). Available online at http://speaker.house.gov/newsroom/pressreleases?id=0031.

———. "Text of Nancy Pelosi's Speech." *San Francisco Chronicle*, January 4, 2007: Available online at http://sfgate.com/cgi-bin/article.cgi?f=/c/a/2007/01/04/BAG5ANCTQ27.DTL.

"Pelosi Says She'll Press on with Armenian 'Genocide' Resolution." CNN, October 14, 2007. Available online at http://www.cnn.com/2007/POLITICS/10/14/us.turkey/index.html.

Phillips, Michael M., Sarah Lueck, and Sudeep Reddy. "Stimulus Deal Spurred by Fears of Voter Backlash." *Wall Street Journal*, January 26–27, 2008, p. A-6.

Powers, John. "House Proud." *Vogue*. Vol. 197 (March 2007): p. 557.

"Pratfall in Damascus." *Washington Post*, April 5, 2007, p. A-16.

Rubin, Trudy. "Why Criticize Pelosi for Bush Mess? Sure, Her Visit to Syria Will Do Nothing Except Possibly Boost Assad, but the Mideast Morass Is the White House's Fault." *Philadelphia Inquirer*, April 8, 2007, p. D-1.

Safire, William. *Safire's Political Dictionary*. New York: Random House, 1992, p. 144.

Simon, Richard. "Cloud Over Corn's Moment in Sun; An Ethanol Mandate, Popular in Farm States, Is Seen as Key to Passing an Energy Bill." *Los Angeles Times*, November 28, 2007, p A-18.

———. "House Passes a Sweeping Energy Bill." *Los Angeles Times*, December 7, 2007, p. A-17.

Steihm, Jamie. "A Look at the Baltimore Roots of the Two Most Powerful Women in Congress." WYPR News, Baltimore, Feb. 18, 2008. Available online at http://www.publicbroadcasting.net/wypr/news.newsmain?action=article&ARTICLE_ID=1228979§ionID=1.

Stern, Yoav. "U.S. Republican Meets Assad Day After Contentious Pelosi Visit." *Haaretz*, April 7, 2007. Available online at http://www.haaretz.com/hasen/spages/845904.html.

Thurman, James N. "Perils of Wielding a Veto Pen." *Christian Science Monitor*. Vol. 90 (June 25, 1998): p. 3.

Tomasky, Michael. "A Trial Would Fail, and Split the U.S. When Unity Behind Progressive Ideas Is Needed." *Philadelphia Inquirer*, January 27, 2008, p. D-1.

Toner, Robin. "Catholic Politicians Confront Public and Private Conscience." *New York Times*, June 25, 1990, p. A-1.

Turner, Robert F. "Illegal Diplomacy." *Wall Street Journal*, April 6, 2007, p. A-10.

Werner, Erica. "Iraq War Losses Cloud Speaker's Year." Associated Press, January 1, 2008. Available online at http://ap.google.com/article/ALeqM5iXRurPqiJaRNLxY3-Rj9wWgVH1vwD8TSV1880.

Zeleny, Jeff. "House Votes to Expand Stem Cell Research." *New York Times*, June 8, 2007, p. A-24.

Zernike, Kate. "A Shift in Power, Starting with 'Madam Speaker.'" *New York Times*, January 24, 2007, p. A-1.

———. "A Chocolate-and-Gavel Leader." *International Herald Tribune*, November 9, 2006. Available online at http://www.iht.com/articles/2006/11/09/news/pelosi.php.

FURTHER RESOURCES

BOOKS

Buly, Cythnia A., editor. *Global Warming: Opposing Viewpoints*. San Diego: Greenhaven Press, 2006.

Carlisle, Rodney P. *Iraq War*. New York: Chelsea House, 2007.

Hamilton, Lee H. *How Congress Works and Why You Should Care*. Bloomington, Ind.: Indiana University Press, 2004.

Kimmer, Patricia K. *Syria*. New York: Children's Press, 2005.

Koestler-Grack, Rachel A. *The House of Representatives*. New York: Chelsea House, 2007.

Marcovitz, Hal. *Nancy Pelosi*. Philadelphia: Chelsea House, 2004.

Remini, Robert V. *The House: The History of the House of Representatives*. New York: HarperCollins Publishers/Smithsonian Books, 2006.

Schichtman, Sandra H. *Nancy Pelosi*. Greensboro, N.C.: Morgan Reynolds, 2007.

WEB SITES

Center for American Women and Politics
http://www.cawp.rutgers.edu/

House Speaker Nancy Pelosi
http://speaker.house.gov/

Thomas: The Library of Congress (Legislative information from the Library of Congress)
http://thomas.loc.gov

United Nations Intergovernmental Panel on Climate Change
http://www.ipcc.ch

United States House of Representatives
http://www.house.gov

INDEX

ABOUT THE AUTHOR

HAL MARCOVITZ is a former journalist who makes his home in Chalfont, Pennsylvania. He has written more than 100 books for young readers, including biographies of civil rights leaders Al Sharpton and Eleanor Holmes Norton, farm labor organizer Cesar Chavez, and film director Ron Howard. His prior biography of Nancy Pelosi, published by Chelsea House in 2004, was named to *Booklist* magazine's list of recommended feminist books for young readers.

PICTURE CREDITS

Page

9: AP Images
15: Dennis Brack/Landov
23: AP Images
29: AP Images
34: AP Images
43: AP Images
54: Roger L. Wollenberg/UPI/Landov
63: AP Images
70: AP Images
80: AP Images
83: Kevin Dietsch/UPI/Landov
89: Greg Whitesell/UPI/Landov
96: AP Images
101: AP Images
109: Kevin Dietsch/UPI/Landov
114: Jack Smith/Bloomberg News/Landov
122: AP Images